CW01189102

Two SILENT NIGHTS times two

By
Esther E. Schmidt & Addy Archer

Copyright © 2022 by Esther E. Schmidt & Addy Archer
All rights reserved.

No part of this book may be reproduced in any form,
without permission in writing from the author.

This book is a work of fiction. Incidents, names, places,
characters and other stuff mentioned in this book is the results
of the author's imagination. Two Silent Nights Times Two is a
work of fiction. If there is any resemblance,
it is entirely coincidental.

This content is for mature audiences only. Please do not read
if sexual situations, violence and explicit language offends you.

Cover design by:
Esther E. Schmidt

Editor #1:
Christi Durbin

Editor #2:
Virginia Tesi Carey

Cover Model:
Kevin R Davis

Photographer:
JW Photography / Jean Woodfin

CHAPTER 01

CONROY

I'm sitting in the corner of the main room of the clubhouse observing everyone. It's Christmas Eve and the majority of the brothers are hanging around and drinking a beer to relax. None of the younger generation has an old lady and they would rather hang here instead of sitting alone in their rooms.

It's been like this for several years for me as well. I used to have an old lady until she passed away. The loss of Maureen still makes my chest constrict at times like this. She was a good woman, a caring mother to our son, Kayler, and the perfect president's old lady.

A deep sigh rips from me. Sometimes I wish I could move on, find another good woman to build a new bond with to subdue the void she left behind. Especially at times like this when we just had weeks of hell with the loss of several brothers due to a rival MC.

We just retaliated, taking out the whole chapter, and it's also why these guys are lounging tonight. They deserve it. I know there are still a few of those rival fucks out there we need to hunt down. Eli for instance, I know the little shit is vicious as fuck. But I'm sure they won't take any action in the near future; they need to regroup before they're able to.

I rub a hand over my face and decide to grab a beer; I need to stop thinking and feeling sorry for myself. It's not like my cock hasn't seen any action, but it has been a while. Somehow none of the women I've met spark anything inside me, not enough to make my cock twitch.

Maybe it's something like overload since we own a strip club and have tits and ass shaking on the tap. Hell, the brothers even arranged a stripper earlier today for Kayler, their VP, to celebrate his birthday. Not just any stripper because my son is very specific in his preferences when it comes to having a woman for entertainment.

Like I mentioned, the club owns a strip club and it's where Kayler developed his addiction. He likes to watch but doesn't touch any woman who lives in or around town. Seems the one they arranged for him is special because I saw him take her out on his bike over an hour ago. A first for him; taking a chick out and putting her on his bike.

Strange to say the least. Fuck. I might be a tad

jealous. Yeah, I definitely need a beer before I drown in my own pity-party. I rise to my feet while at the same time the door of the clubhouse swings open. My son steps inside and whips his head around as if he's searching for something.

The stripper woman he put on the back of his bike tonight punches him in the gut and I hear Kayler mutter, "What the actual fuck?"

"Answer my damn question, asshole," the woman snaps. "Why the hell did I just experience a fucking drive by shooting?"

A what? I'm striding across the room with my next breath.

Standing before Kayler, I demand, "What's she talking about?"

"I told you this wasn't over," he growls at me. "Eli was hanging out of a car, firing bullets at us. He probably followed me from the clubhouse and was waiting for us to get out of the diner. Which fucking means–"

"He linked this woman to you because you've never had someone warming your back," I finish for him.

"Oh no," the woman whispers from beside Kayler. "Does that mean he knows who I am? If so, does that mean my sister and my nephew are both at risk as well? They seriously don't need this added to the shit that was thrown at their feet. Dammit."

I narrow my eyes, hating the fact innocents were pulled into our mess, especially a woman with a kid who clearly has other stuff to deal with.

"What shit was thrown at your sister's feet?" I question.

Her shoulders drop. "Her ex just traded her in for his five years younger secretary. They ran off together to Paris, Hawaii, or who the hell knows because he cleared out their entire bank account. Did I mention he left his own freaking son behind? Not that he ever cared about the kid and has always been an asshole to the both of them. Ugh. She should have left him sooner. Then that loan shark wouldn't have forced Bo's debt on her and I wouldn't be here making sure that fucker got the five grand they don't even fucking owe because it's Bo's debt." By now she's roaring out her words but instantly falls silent, a look of defeat slides across her face.

"Take a deep breath, sweetheart, all will be fine," I order and let my eyes slide to my son. "You want to take point on this, or shall I?"

His gaze is still on the woman beside him. I've seen that look. Felt it bloom deep in my bones. It's the prospect of something new and enticing, a foundation for something greater. Something I once had and let it evolve to love…something I lost the day his mother died.

"Olcay's on lockdown and I want everyone sober and on their fucking toes until the rest of those fuckers are dead or handled," Kayler snaps. "And I want Eli's head on a platter for putting my woman at risk."

"Your woman, eh?" I question, surprised he's jumping the gun on his emotions because he's always cool and collected.

I guess he's aware of his feelings, the ones I noticed when he was staring at her. Kayler takes a few breaths and I can tell he's putting things in order inside his head and see his claim before I hear the actual claim.

"My woman," he states loud and clear for the whole clubhouse to hear.

I smack his shoulder. "Congratulations, son. Now." I turn my attention to Olcay. "I'm going to need your sister's address. From now on your problems are club business and this shit with a loan shark redirecting a fucking debt to a single mother doesn't fly in my book so I'm going to take point on that one."

"Her ex didn't pay the rent and they were evicted on the day he left with his secretary. Odette and Baxter are living with me now."

"Address, sweetheart," I repeat.

Olcay rattles out her address and I turn to face Kayler. "I'm going to handle the sister part and will bring her and the kid to the clubhouse in case Eli finds out who your old lady is. You're going to get everyone up to speed and handle everything here, VP. Church tomorrow morning bright and early." My attention slides back to Olcay and I hold out my hand. "Keys, please. And call your sister so she knows I'm coming."

She digs her keys out of her pocket and hands them over, then stalks over to the corner with her phone for some privacy.

"I hope to fuck her sister is older and shares her good looks," I murmur.

My son shakes his head. "What the hell, Dad? You can't be serious? You heard what the woman just went through. She has a kid for fuck's sake."

I merely shrug. "I made, raised, and tolerate you. I think I can handle it."

He rubs a hand over his face and doesn't respond.

Olcay joins us again. "She knows you're coming to talk about her ex and the loan shark. I didn't mention anything about what just happened."

"Appreciate it," I grunt and stalk out the door without another word.

Instead of taking my bike, I jump into my truck and drive in the direction of the address Olcay gave me. If her sister has a fraction of this chick's beauty it'll be no burden at all to keep an eye on them.

Though, I don't consider it a burden to stand up for a woman who has been kicked to the curb in a fucked-up way, along with her damn kid for fuck's sake. That shit doesn't fly in my book. The minor chance of the club's threat spilling over to her isn't very big but I'm not taking any risks with the stuff this woman went through.

I come to a stop in front of a building with bold letters on the windows stating it's a dance studio. Jumping out of my truck, I glance up at the apartment above it. There's a dim light flashing through the window, must be from a TV. The door opens a crack before I have a chance to ring the doorbell.

"Are you a biker?" a stern voice asks through the small opening the chain allows.

I have no clue what face belongs to the voice because the hallway she's standing in is dark.

"Open the door, Odette," I rumble.

"Answer the damn question first or you'll see this door slam shut," she fires back.

The corner of my mouth twitches. "I've been the president of Silver Rain MC for decades, been a biker for a fuckton longer. Now open the damn door, Detta."

I hear the chain and my mouth twitches some more with the hint of a laugh, knowing I riled her up by twisting her name.

The door swings open and she jabs a finger against my chest while whisper-hissing in a harsh tone. "You could have just said yes instead of using a stupid nickname you bikers are known for using."

"Where's the fun in that?" I question and lean in closer to her face to rile her up some more when I add, "Detta."

"It's Odette." She spins around and points at the stairs leading up. "Be quiet. My son is sleeping and I really want him to have a good night's sleep after the day we had."

I dip my chin and stalk past her. As I take the stairs up to the apartment I hear her lock the door with a deadbolt. The living room is attached to an open kitchen and it's surprisingly big.

"Did you come to get the money and deliver it to the loan shark?" Detta asks from behind me.

I slowly turn and take in the short, explosive woman standing before me in the dim light the TV offers. Her brown eyes are locked on mine, dark blonde hair is framing her face, the tips brushing her shoulders.

Wide hips, firm legs with calves that show definition. Her reindeer print shorts are hanging low on her waist and due to the off-shoulder shirt that matches her shorts, there's a hint of her soft belly showing.

She slightly spins to close the door to the stairs and damn…I'd like to bounce my cock off that lush ass. Great. Now I'm sporting a hard-on. I forgot what a real woman looked like with all the tight frames coming and going in the strip club and clubhouse.

"Nice PJs," I remark to hopefully drag her attention to my face so she won't notice the bulge growing against my zipper. "Do you have a thing for reindeer?"

She glances down and shrugs. "It's Christmas Eve. Santa, also known as my sister, gave them to me. I can't afford to be picky when I only packed one change of clothes and some underwear."

"Let me guess, you packed a shitload for the kid, prioritizing the way a mother does."

A deep breath flows from her, and she stalks to the couch to sit down and curls her legs under that fine ass of hers. "Sure did. But it still wasn't enough…we basically have nothing. At least thanks to Olcay we have a roof over our head when she took us in. I still can't believe she accepted Babette's offer to take over a dancing side gig in honor of your son's birthday so we can pay the loan shark to get him off my back."

I shake my head and take the seat across from the couch. "No way in hell are we going to pay that fucker. That debt isn't yours; I'm going to remind the fucker of that little detail and let him know not to fuck with you."

"Now wait a damn minute," she snaps.

My eyes slide to the hallway and back. "Keep it down, you wanted your kid to get his sleep. Besides, whatever you have to say about the loan shark falls on a deaf man's ears; no discussion. I'm going to handle it and make sure you and the kid are safe."

"Why?" She narrows her eyes. "Why would you do that for a couple of strangers? Because something tells me you're not a man who does something out of the goodness of his heart."

I fake shock and grab for my heart. "Damn, woman, you're cruel. Also, very observant. Let's just say I'll make you a deal."

She jolts to her feet. "If you think I'm going to bounce my tits and sway my ass in your face in exchange for your help, you're insane. My sister might have agreed to do a one-time deal to entertain your son, but no way will I be so much as tempted to…to–"

"Shake your tits and ass in my face," I conveniently finish for her, liking the visual that's now planted inside my head. "Shame. Though, that's not what I was going to suggest."

"Oh." Her ass hits the couch. "Sorry. I just assumed...yikes. You probably have an old lady–"

I cut her off right there, hating the reminder when I'm standing here with a damn hard-on. "My wife died over five years ago."

Sincerity clouds her face when she softly murmurs, "I'm so sorry. I didn't mean to bring up your loss."

"None taken," I gruffly reply.

"What was the deal you wanted to offer?" she questions, quickly turning back at the discussion on hand.

And fuck if I can't voice the deal I had thought up inside my head. Voicing how I'd like to fuck her into the new year doesn't sound right when we just mentioned my dead old lady. Yet somehow my cock is still hard.

"No deal," I find myself saying. "My son just claimed your sister as his old lady. You being her sister makes this shit club business and as the president, I'll make sure the loan shark disappears. Just give me the rundown of all the information you have when it comes to your ex and the shit he was in, and I'll handle it."

Her eyes are locked on mine and I get the feeling she's sizing me up.

A few heartbeats later she blurts, "No."

"No?" I grunt. "What the fuck, no?"

"I'm not a charity case or taking free rides just because my sister has a new boyfriend." She jabs her chin up a notch and I'm loving the feisty look and defiance in her voice when she says, "Name your price so we can make a deal that's just between us and not connected to my sister or anyone else."

I guess getting my cock wet is back on the table again…as are the fireworks I'm sure are bound to follow when I get a taste of this feisty woman.

Two Silent Nights

CHAPTER 02

DETTA

His piercing, stormy gray eyes flaring with lust pin me in place. Every move this man makes is calculated. There is no jumping in head-first the way Bo, my ex, would do for instance, but that cheating asshole was always selfish and reckless.

Maybe it's the age difference. This man standing before me with his gray-streaked beard gives the impression he knows what life has to give and will act accordingly after he calculated the risk. Clearly a huge difference from my idiot ex who couldn't care less about anything other than himself.

Hell, this stranger before me is ready to swoop in and take care of the mess I'm in due to my ex just because my sister jumped into a relationship with his son. My sister. His son. My mind is blown when I realize my nipples are pushing against the fabric of my shirt all because of the silver fox standing before me.

My body is reacting to a man who is clearly many years older than I am. Crazy considering I was just dumped and landed face-first into a load of problems. All while my mind is now overtaken by desire for this rugged biker.

"Can you cook?" he grunts, and I have to blink twice to process his change in topic.

"Cook? Yes, I can. Why?" I wonder.

He crosses his arms in front of his chest and my eyes slide to his forearms. They are defined and his right one is covered with a brightly colored flower surrounded by shading. Shit. Why am I ogling him?

My eyes snap back to his and I notice the smirk on his face when he rumbles, "Here's the deal. You're in a tight spot due to your ex, something you definitely didn't ask for or need with a tiny kid to take care of. You've moved in with your sister, not exactly an ideal, long-term situation either."

I slowly nod, knowing he's right so far.

"Ever since my wife died my house is empty as fuck and I haven't had a good home-cooked meal in forever. How about you and the kid each take a room and keep me company for as long as you need while feeding me in exchange? I'll provide the groceries but you need to do the work of feeding the three of us. You living under my roof also means you're my responsibility and therefore I will handle the shit you're wrapped in. Sound good?"

"Keep you company," I murmur while my heart skips a beat and my body fills with excitement as I read between the lines.

Dammit, it's been too long since I've had sex. I suspected Bo was cheating on me and the way we were going head-to-head at every turn didn't leave for much sex or closeness the past four months.

I went as far as getting myself tested to make sure he didn't give me an STD as I was taking steps to leave him. I should have done it sooner because he threw me in a whirlwind of a fucked-up mess before I could, leaving me with nothing.

"Yeah. Fill the house with voices, the scent of food, making it alive instead of letting it eat away at me with the silence and cold it's drowning with now." His voice takes a husky undertone when he adds, "I'll take anything extra you have for me, though. But rest assured it won't be part of the deal. It would just be something between me and you."

I glance over my shoulder to make sure my son isn't standing there, even if he's a sound sleeper. "Something between me and you. Sex. You're talking about having sex, right?"

He steps closer and lowers his head until his lips brush my ear. "I'm talking about wrapping your young pussy around my cock to make me feel the life your body is filled with. I've gone too long without release. And when you opened that door, throwing sass at me before I even so much as stepped over that threshold, all I wanted to do was bury myself balls deep until you come so many times, your voice is simply hoarse from screaming my name."

Clearly the bottom pair of slutty lips take over the top ones when I blurt without thinking, "We should definitely have sex then."

A feral grin slides over his face. "Great. I don't know what I would have done if you refused the deal. Sure as fuck would I have helped you clear up the mess your scumbag ex made. Though, it would have been a damn shame not to taste you."

I have no clue why my body is reacting so strongly to this man. A perfect stranger, way older than me, and so different from the men I've wasted myself on in my life. It's crazy how every word coming from this man vibrates through me in ripples that draw out pleasure.

What am I thinking? My life is a mess and I should be focused on my son and how to move forward. Yet, at this moment, many would deem me selfish but the past few days, hell…months…have shattered my life to pieces and I've been holding my chin high for the sake of my kid.

Right now all I want to do is hit pause on life and throw myself in a sea of pleasure. If only for a few minutes that would be a welcome distraction to the shitty havoc that's called my life. Why not give in?

My son is a sound sleeper and will sleep through the night. The man is clearly offering. We're both willing, both adults, and both have needs. The days filled with misery, frustration, pain, guilt, disaster, and all kinds of other fucked-up things have been dragging my spirits and energy. I deserve something good, right? Hell, I might be trying to boost myself into something I want but I also need this, dammit.

"Why wait to have a taste?" I boldly state, deciding I should take what I want.

Hell, how many chances does a woman get to give in to what feels right with a man who lights your body the way it's never been lit? Never. That's how many chances in life I've had when it comes to good men in my life. And he looks real damn fine. Shit.

Bo was a string of bad decisions and it led to an unexpected pregnancy, tying us together ever since. Baxter turned out to be the best part of my life but his father? Everything was a struggle. Another reminder I should have left sooner, my fault.

"Right now," the man growls and doesn't even make it sound like a question, more like an agreement.

"Right now," I agree, mentally cheering myself for taking a shower and shaving before changing into my pajamas earlier. "Do you have a condom?"

His eyes hit the ceiling and he groans loud in frustration. "Aw, fuck. I don't. Those youngsters might carry condoms in their back pocket and wallet but I haven't felt the need to fuck in a real long damn time so I don't bother to carry rubbers."

"Dammit," I grumble.

"I'm clean, though." He grabs his phone and

thumbs the screen before holding it out for me to see. "See? I had a recent physical done. My son always does one right before his birthday and he drags me along to do the same."

I give him a nod. "I'm clean too. When I suspected Bo was cheating on me, I had a full checkup done. I had a sterilization a year after Baxter was born."

"Fucking bare it is." Satisfaction drips from every word and I swear I feel the rumble of his voice brushing my nipples.

Dammit, that's just nonsense. I can't feel his voice, right? I'm going to blame it on the moment because there's no way my body is reacting to this man; it's been too long and I need to have sex and get it over with. A release will clear my body of both the need to have this man and the stress of what I went through. Then I can move on and focus.

I hold my finger up. "Hold that thought. I'm going to check on my son and lock his room to make sure he can't walk in on us. I'm sure he will sleep through the night unless we get too loud but we're going to keep it down, agreed?"

His mouth turns into a flat line. "I'd rather make you scream but I understand tonight will need to be different."

"Good. I'll be right back." I whirl around and rush down the hall and come to a stop in front of the room my son is sleeping in.

I peek inside and my heart stutters at the sight of his peacefully sleeping face. His wild dark blond hair, similar to mine, is standing on end. What the hell am I going to do? I have a steady job as an ER nurse, but it will take time to regroup and get enough money to let the both of us land on our feet.

That is if there aren't any more surprises thrown at my feet the way the loan shark dropped my ex's five grand worth of debt on me. Also…what the hell am I doing with this complete stranger waiting for me to have sex while my son is in here sleeping?

My throat clogs and I have no clue how to move forward from here on out. I'm stuck between a rock and a hard place and I don't think I can worm my way out of this, even if I had all the lube in the world. I squeeze my eyes shut and take a deep breath.

My eyes flash open when I feel a hard body pressing against my back and a soft voice that says, "Come on, Detta. Leave the kid's door open 'cause I can tell you're not ready for what we both want. It will happen when the time is right, just not right now, okay?"

Dammit. Disappointment and relief flood my senses all at the same time. When I'm unable to so much as move, Conroy wraps a strong arm around my waist and pulls me out of the room, making sure the door stays slightly ajar.

"You want coffee or something stronger?" he asks and is standing in the kitchen within a few strides.

I follow him and sink down onto one of the chairs. Placing my elbows on the table I take my head in my hands and mutter, "Coffee, please."

"Why don't you start from the beginning, how you landed your sexy ass here with your sister? That way we can get to know one another." I hear a snort and then he says, "I'll start and you can wait for some coffee and share after I'm done."

I lift my head from my hands to glance at the man's back as he moves through the kitchen.

Without looking back, he rumbles, "Maureen and I met at a diner across town. She was a waitress and the first time I saw her I asked her out but her father wouldn't let her." He glances over his shoulder. "I was born into this MC, my father was the president before me so at the age of barely twenty I knew I was going to be the next in line to take over. I showed up the next day, and the next, and kept going until she agreed to go out. Knocked her up to make sure we were tied together, nine months later Kayler was born. I knew she was it for me. Call it a gut instinct, chemistry, or whatever…I just knew. We were happy for over twenty years…then she died. Heart attack."

He places two cups of coffee on the table and sits down. "No background, no family issues or medical…whatever. She had a heart attack that caused irreversible damage, had another one in the ambulance and was pronounced dead when she arrived at the hospital."

I reach out and cover my hand with his. "I'm so sorry."

He bobs his head. "It's been five years."

"Any span of time doesn't lessen the pain of losing someone dear," I murmur. "Especially when they are ripped from you without any notice."

The flash of grief is there one moment and then it's gone.

He clears his voice and asks, "Need any sugar or cream?"

I give him a small smile. "No thanks, black as tar is fine by me." I take a deep breath and confess, "Bo and I met and I got knocked up the same day. We decided to move in together. I had a steady job, he was dabbling in underground boxing matches and wanted to slow down. Fewer games, more future. He saw becoming a parent as an indicator to get his shit together." A rude, unfeminine snort rips from me. "Right. All lies as it turns out because he never gave a shit about becoming a parent when Baxter was born and ran off almost five years later. He cleaned out our bank accounts and borrowed money from a loan shark on top of it. He didn't pay the mortgage which got us evicted the day he left which he knew was coming because he planned it all."

I take a sip of coffee and as I swallow and stare into the black liquid I add, "I knew he was cheating on me. Hell, I got myself tested to make sure he didn't gamble with my health and I was going to take steps to leave him but clearly, I was too late. Now there's nothing left and I have to start from scratch. The timing sucks and being thrown out on my ass stings even more to know he dumped me and ran off with a chick years younger than me. No stretch marks, tight ass and belly, I bet. Ugh. I should be glad I'm rid of the asshole who was a good-for-nothing father who hardly spent time with or managed any attention when it came to Baxter. Every shift I had I'd either had to take him with me to the daycare at work or arrange for a sitter because Bo couldn't take care of the kid. His words, not mine. He called his own son 'the kid' more than calling him by his damn name."

I rub my temples and grumble, "I shouldn't badmouth him. Karma will bite him in the ass soon enough."

"What job do you have if they have a daycare?" Conroy asks.

A proud smile tugs my lips. "ER nurse."

His eyes widen a fraction and he nods, appreciation lacing his voice when he says, "Honorable job but a fucking hard one. I know all too well about the killer shifts. My mother used to be an ER nurse. Shame she isn't alive anymore, pretty sure she would have loved to have met you."

Again, I reach out to cover his hand with mine. Our eyes lock and I can't break away. His heat seeps into mine through our skin and I'm pretty damn sure if my ovaries still functioned I would be walking away pregnant by this man.

Our connection and shared moments of life align us perfectly. If age is just a number, lust an emotion to act on, and happiness fleeting…then what the hell is stopping us from taking a leap if it feels this good?

32 Two Silent Nights

CHAPTER 03

CONROY

"Here you go, Champ," I tell Baxter, Detta's four-year-old son, and place a plate with a freshly cooked waffle in front of him.

He eagerly pulls his plate closer. "Thank you," he murmurs, eying the food as if it's a prize he just won but then his head whips up and he blurts, "Champ?"

The corner of my mouth twitches. "Yeah, Champ. You know, like a champion. Any man who rises early and is as cheerful as a hummingbird is a champion who seizes the day in my book."

I must say, it's quite refreshing to be woken up by a kid poking his finger against my beard, asking if I'm Santa's helper and forgot to wear a Santa suit. He was grinning ear to ear as if he was telling a joke. Then he asked if I knew if there was food because he was hungry.

My own son is twenty-five so it's been a while since I've been in the presence of a four-year-old, but Baxter is quite the sunny and cheerful little man. Except for the poking my beard part 'cause I sure as fuck don't like to be compared to Santa when I have the hots for the little dude's mom.

He spears a piece of waffle on his fork. "A champ, like you." He shoves the food in his mouth and chews fast. "Yum!" he squeaks and starts to inhale the rest of his waffle.

I chuckle and open the waffle iron to take out the next one and throw some batter in there for a new one. "I don't know about that, Champ. Normally I ain't cheerful. I guess you bring out the best in me."

Turning, I place a plate on the table and notice Detta standing in the middle of the living room, eyes locked on her kid.

Lifting my chin in her direction I rumble, "Look who decided to join us and check out that smile tugging her lovely mouth."

Baxter's head whips to the left. "Mommy! Come. Conroy made waffles."

She strolls our way. "If they taste so much as a hint of what this divine scent is filling the whole house, I'm in for a treat."

"They're yummy," Baxter mumbles, his mouth full of waffle.

Detta places a kiss on the top of his head and takes a seat. She looks much better than she did yesterday. I'm guessing sleep treated her well. After our long talk at the kitchen table, we watched some TV. She fell asleep and when I carried her to bed she murmured about needing to be up early for Baxter.

When I assured her I could watch him she murmured something about me being the number one on her list to Santa. I'm sure she was sleep drunk, but it was cute as fuck for sure. I'm glad she was able to catch up on some much-needed sleep.

I place a mug of steaming coffee in front of her along with a waffle and regain my seat across from them.

"Thanks." The smile tugging her lips is as genuine and as gorgeous as the twinkle in her brown eyes.

"You're welcome," I grunt, trying like hell to focus on my own coffee so I can ignore the growing hard-on I'm sporting under the table.

Talk about screwed up timing with her son sitting right across from me. Somehow the thought of this single mother being tied to a young child doesn't bother me. It should be with me being forty-five and already done raising my own kid who is twenty-five for fuck's sake.

Yet here I am, hoping she didn't change her mind about what we agreed upon yesterday.

It's as if she can read my mind when she says, "Does your offer still stand? I mean, it's a lot…taking in the two of us and I would absolutely understand if–"

I eagerly cut her off with, "The offer still stands."

Again, with the smile that makes her breathtaking and in my opinion needs to stay on her face instead of the dark smudges under her eyes and the worry lines she was sporting last night.

"I already called Kayler and let him know I'm handling everything concerning the both of you. He's going to take lead on club business for now so I can focus on you guys. We'll finish breakfast and throw your stuff in my truck. The both of you can check out my house and if there's anything we need we can get it tomorrow when the stores are open. I have enough groceries stocked so we'll be fine for now."

Baxter's gaze bounces between his mother and me, eyes filled with a loaded expression but his lips stay sealed shut.

"Sounds good. But I am going to make sure to repay you for everything you do," she fiercely tells me.

"No need to remind me," I mutter. "Besides, maybe Champ here can help me out in the backyard. The last storm left a bunch of small branches all over the place."

"I can help," Baxter blurts. "I'm good at picking up stuff, right Mom?"

She smiles down at him. "Yeah, you are."

"Are we going to Conroy's house? Stay there instead of with Auntie Olcay?"

Detta gives him a firm nod. "Yes–"

A loud cheer from Baxter cuts off her words but she laughs from the way the little man pumps his fists into the air.

"Well, I don't have to ask if you're okay with it, huh?" Her eyes twinkle when she says, "Seeing as you already finished your waffle, why don't you go to your room and make sure to pack your bag?"

"Yes, Mom," Baxter quips and slides off his chair.

He takes his plate and puts it on the kitchen counter before speed walking in the direction of the room.

"Clean up after yourself and no running in the house," I mutter. "You raised him well."

She releases an unfeminine snort. "Only when he remembers, and like now when he's happy and excited about something so he's on his best behavior. Just wait till you're around us a little while longer. You'll want to plaster him behind the wallpaper or flush him down the toilet. He has quite the temper, not to mention the force of a tornado when it comes to littering his toys all over the place. Besides, I'm not really letting him pack his bag, he's four, he'll probably stash it with toys and nothing else."

"I already raised a son, remember? He was the epitome of a pain in the ass, reminded him of that little fact this morning as well. I ain't a damn rookie. I can handle anything, Detta." I lean back in my chair and cross my arms in front of my chest. "I'm also the president of an MC filled with brothers I keep in line no matter what lands on our plate."

"Thank you." She shoots a quick look over her shoulder in the direction of the hallway when she adds, "I'm actually glad you're stepping up to help us. Not that I'm ungrateful for what my sister is doing but if I'm being honest? The loan shark and what else Bo left us with is a heavy weight on my shoulders, something I don't want to put on hers. I mean, what if there's more? I know the underground fighting he was active in when we met evolved into him organizing them. Something I only recently became aware of. What if others will come looking for us because they can't get a hold of him? It's a terrifying thought."

"No one is going to hurt you or the boy," I fiercely vow. "My son will also keep your sister at the clubhouse, so we have the both of you covered while it gives us a chance to look into everything, okay?"

"Okay." A choppy sigh rips from her. "With my life being flipped upside-down I was forced to take some days off work. Thankfully I was able to when I explained the situation. It did help that I never take a sick day and have worked my ass off for years."

"Then I'd say you're past due some well-deserved vacation time."

She points her fork at the last bite of waffle left on her plate. "I will make the next breakfast and dinner but I do hope I get to enjoy more of these amazing waffles."

"It's been a while since I made them. Hell, I think Kayler was a teenager the last time he asked me to make them for him." I rub the back of my neck and feel a hint of a smile tugging my lips.

"They are truly amazing and if you don't mind, I'd like to have your recipe." She winces. "I'm probably not as good as you because I suck at making pancakes or anything that involves whipping up a batter from scratch. I'm a good cook, though."

"I'm the other way around, not great at cooking dinner but I manage. It's the pancakes, waffles, and cookies I'm good at. Spending time watching and helping Maureen taught me as much." The last part slips out and I shut my big mouth.

What the hell am I thinking rattling on about another woman? I'm sure it's not something she wants to hear. Especially when I want to bury myself between her legs.

"I'm sure you miss her a lot," she softly says.

I bob my head and rub the ink on my forearm.

"The flower, is it something special you had done for her?" she asks and my eyes collide with Detta's.

Brown and warm, such a stark contrast to the blue Maureen had. These two are such a contradiction it would be impossible to compare them, and I like this little fact. Mainly because no woman should be compared to another but especially since each person is damn unique.

"Yeah," I find myself saying. "No one knows but I think my son suspects since I got the ink on the day she was buried. An everlasting flower for the woman who branded herself into my past while she is vacant in my future."

"That's beautiful and yet so sad," she whispers

and the both of us fall silent as we stare at one another.

I clear my throat to make my voice sound firm because she needs to understand, "I never gave it one single damn thought…till now. Didn't think I'd want or needed to say this…but I'm ready to move forward. I'm not stuck or hung up on the past."

She reaches across the table and wraps her fingers around my wrist and gives me a tiny squeeze. With sass in her voice she says, "I kinda got the memo when you made the offer, both to taste me and the moving in part." She pulls back and takes her warmth with her. "If it was just me, I'd jump into your arms without thinking but I have a responsibility–"

I know where this is going so I take over the discussion. "Baxter. He's also the reason why I'm stepping up. The way you were kicked to the curb along with that boy rubs me the wrong way. So, it's not only your responsibility, mine as well. I will make sure to keep the two of you safe, even if that fucker of an ex of yours shows up again."

Her eyes widen with horror. "I hope not. I don't want anything to do with him and I don't want him anywhere near Baxter. He never showed any interest in him anyway. I should call a lawyer, and get things in motion to make sure…shit. I don't even know what to do."

Now I'm the one reaching over the table to grab her hand. "Like I said, my responsibility as well. For now, you're going to put everything on hold because there's nothing else to do since it's Christmas and everything is closed. After the holidays I will reach out to our lawyer and get things up and running. The two of you staying with me will also keep you safe because we don't have a connection. Checking out your sister's place is the first place Bo or anyone who knows him will look. Besides, my house is located behind the clubhouse and security is tight."

Her delicate hand covers mine. "Sounds like a plan."

"I'm ready," Baxter quips.

A thought crosses my mind and I whisper, "Any chance I can let the kid ride my son's old mini bike? I think it's still buried in the back of the shed, but I have no clue if it's still up and running. He might have to help me tweak the thing, not sure if I can get it going but if I do there's a helmet and such in the shed somewhere too."

Her eyes light up. "Are you kidding me? He would love the attention and work, I'm sure of it."

"Then I guess we have a small project we can get our hands dirty with." I grin and she shoots me one right back.

"Mom? Did you pack your bag?" Baxter asks.

She turns and stalks toward him. Placing a kiss on the top of his head she says, "I'm going to do that right now. Why don't you help Conroy with cleaning up? I've heard he has something he wants to talk to you about."

Baxter eagerly nods and speed walks my way while Detta heads for the hallway. She stops to glance at us, and I know the look she's wearing. I've seen it in Maureen's eyes when she used to look at Kayler.

It's a mother's look. One where wishes are displayed with an edge of fear combined with longing. Wanting to reach for the stars for your kid while building a safety net to make sure he's able to fall if they set the bar too high.

This woman is a gem, warming my chest with her every move and action. I hate the shit she's wrapped it but on the other hand? If Bo didn't kick her to the curb I would still be empty-handed while now I'm itching to fill said hands with this woman.

CHAPTER 04

DETTA

I take a moment to stare down at my son who is sleeping in his new room for the time being. It's a teenage boy's room and I have to smile at the reminder of Conroy showing us the room before jolting forward and quickly ripping down a few posters of naked women teenage Kayler clearly left behind.

He did mention his son moved into the clubhouse when he was seventeen, leaving the room as it was with only the cleaning lady entering every now and then. The exact same way as the other rooms and it shows the man only comes here to sleep.

Probably because of the reason he mentioned when he offered for us to come live with him; it's a big house but it's empty and silent. Conroy mostly spends his time at the clubhouse, which is normal I guess with him being the president of the MC.

I make sure Baxter is tucked in before I sneak out of the room. The little man is sound asleep and was ready for his nap over an hour ago, but he didn't want to miss one single minute of his time with Conroy.

Who could blame him? When we arrived at Conroy's home earlier today he took my son straight to the shed in the back of his yard where he pulled out a mini bike. Sadly enough it didn't run but they spent hours together trying to fix it.

Conroy was wearing a baseball cap and at some point, when I went to get them some lemonade, Baxter was wearing it. He's still clutching it in his hand while he's sound asleep. Baxter is completely enthralled by Conroy and even if this Christmas has been blown to shit somehow it's turning out to be the best one ever.

There's a huge grin on my face when I stroll into the living room.

"Big man sleeping?" Conroy asks as he stalks my way, offering me a bottle of water.

I twist the cap off and take a few sips. "Out like a light. Thank you. I keep saying it but you have no clue how much it means to both of us. The time you spent with Baxter today was precious. Sadly enough I have to admit that those hours were more than his own father ever gave him. It's probably why he practically inhaled the attention."

"His father's an asshole who doesn't appreciate what's right under his nose. His loss and I hope he realizes soon enough what he lost. Though, I hope you won't take him back. Shitty 'cause that boy sleeping under this roof needs his father." He shakes his head. "Some people just function differently. Tweaking the mini bike today was a welcome flashback to the past for me. I used to take Kayler into the backyard all the time to get our hands dirty with grease. Fixing bikes is what I grew up with as well. My dad did it with me as I did with my son. It's a way to discuss shit if there's a problem or just an escape to skip the pressure and responsibilities of life. Not so much fixing bikes but fixing the mind along with it, you know?"

"That right there," I croak. "Meaningful and so important nowadays. The patience you showed him today was also refreshing. I've told my sister that Bo leaving maybe wasn't such a bad thing. Hell, I was in the middle of getting things in order to leave him because I knew very well things couldn't go on the way they did in our house. The cheating was one thing, disrespecting me, treating me like shit but it was mostly the way he treated Baxter. You, on the other hand, never once lost your patience with Baxter today. Even after a million questions, some of those asked on repeat. You explained everything, some not even making sense to me but he sucked it all up."

Conroy chuckles. "We could work on the bike tomorrow and the next day, along with the day after that, and he'll still be popping the same questions.

Kayler was the same way. Wait till his ass is on that bike and he gets to ride it, then he'll really start to rattle and fill those walls in his room with posters of bikes."

"I really hope so. And thanks again for–"

"Enough," Conroy barks, cutting me off. "No more. I know you're thankful but I'm getting enough out of our deal as well, remember? My house is alive again, you're making dinner, and the old shit from my own son that was rusting and dusting away is put to use again. It's as if our lives were supposed to cross." His voice turns husky. "Of course, I hope in time you'll be warming my bed but that's not part of the deal we made."

A jolt of lust tingles through my veins. "If in time means later tonight…" I shrug as if I'm okay with now or later but I'm actually just as eager as he is.

Last night I was all for jumping this man's bones on the spot but put a pin in my own lusty eagerness due to Baxter. Seeing Conroy spend most of the day giving his full attention to my son without any complaint or frustration. He's shown patience and a male influence that's been lacking from Baxter's life from the day he was born.

It's as if I've been pressed with my nose onto the fact that I should be thanking the stars on my bare knees Bo left us. Another reminder I was doing the right thing by leaving and I should have done it sooner.

All of it is in the past now but meeting this man

also shows I have a lot more to explore in the future. Starting with what it would feel like to surrender my body to this man. He's very different than Bo and the few other men I had encounters with before I fell pregnant with Baxter.

Conroy is older, mature, knows what he wants, and isn't afraid to speak his mind. He also doesn't jump on instinct and was the one who hit the brakes when I had doubts about having sex. Add the fact I'm completely attracted to him and given my situation, I'm allowed to indulge in the pleasure this man is offering.

I have no clue how long this will last or if we have a future together but overthinking is not something I will do on Christmas Day. Especially not when the heavy weight that was thrown on my shoulders when Bo kicked my life to shit is finally being lifted by the help of this man.

Conroy steps forward and closes the distance between us. He reaches for my face with both hands, gathering me close to brush his lips softly against mine. Tentative. My breath catches from the contact.

His tongue breaches my mouth and swoops in to swirl against mine. I groan at the way this man manages to make my body tingle from a mere kiss. I dig my fingers into the sleeveless denim shirt he's wearing to pull him closer.

I could keep kissing this man for hours but the ringing of a phone interrupts our moment. Conroy breaks our kiss but instantly places his forehead against mine. He's breathing hard, showing this kiss affected him just as much as the lustful havoc it caused in me.

"Fuck, woman. You taste like wifey material and now that I've gotten a taste I don't think I'll able to let you go."

His words should make me run. Hell, I was just kicked out of a bad relationship but dammit...this feels right. I have no clue how to answer him or how to react for that matter.

There's no need when he murmurs, "Gotta take this call, sweets. Then I gotta have that mouth again."

This time I'm nodding as he pulls away and reaches for his phone.

"Yeah?" Conroy rumbles.

He listens for a few heartbeats and by the serious and worried look sliding across his face, I'd say the person on the other side of the line isn't giving him good news.

"Be right there. Send Xayne to my house," he grunts and hangs up.

His eyes land on me as he shoves his phone back into his pocket. "My son was stabbed. He's on his way to the clubhouse now. We normally have a doctor who we call but he's out of the country. Would you be able to check him out and stitch him up?"

I grit my teeth. "Nurse and doctor are two different professions. I'm an ER nurse and cannot do stitches simply because it's basically a minor surgical procedure. That being said...Bo's underground fighting most times led to cuts that needed stitches, wounds, and different other injuries. The doctor they had at the events asked me to help out since I was a nurse and needed for me to stitch and handle other things to make it easier on him. I stopped when Baxter was born. Again, I'm an ER nurse, he should go to a hospital."

"He's coming here," Conroy states, and his voice doesn't hold any room for arguments.

"Fine. How bad? I'm not going to risk his life. A minor cut I can stitch but I won't treat him if I'm risking his life," I huff.

"Dunno how bad," he grunts. "I'm gonna ask one of the club brothers to come watch over Baxter and then we can both head over to the clubhouse. Are you okay with that?"

"I'm assuming you know and trust this man because I'd be leaving the only precious link to this world that's tied to my heart. Right next to my sister but she's responsible for herself."

"Your son will be safe and unharmed. The brother I'll have watching over Baxter has been a part of my MC for a decade," Conroy vows.

I nod and at the same time there's a soft knock. Conroy stalks to the door and opens it. There's a guy in his late thirties, neatly shaved along with a buzzcut, holding out his hand for me to shake.

"The name is Xayne," he rumbles.

I give him a firm shake and release his hand when I say, "Odette. My son, Baxter, is taking a nap in the room down the hall. He should be sleeping for at least another hour or two but if he wakes? You call Conroy and I'll be right there, understand?"

"Understood, ma'am." He gives me a firm nod as if I'm his superior who just gave him an order.

I follow Conroy out the door. It's a three-minute walk to the clubhouse and when we enter the main room I see who I'm guessing is Kayler sitting on the couch while my sister is already cleaning the wound.

"What happened?" I ask when I come to a stop next to my sister.

I grab a pair of gloves from the fully stocked medical kit lying open on the table behind her.

I bat Olcay's hands away. "Let me check the wound. Did you sterilize–"

"Yes, I did and have everything laid out behind you. Tell me what you need," Olcay says.

"I'd rather you tell me what the fuck is going on with you two," Kayler snaps.

"Watch your tone," Conroy rumbles from beside Kayler.

I keep my focus on attending to the man's wounds while Olcay assists me.

"Odette's an ER nurse. She also used to fix up her ex when he came home from fighting since the fucker was an underground boxer," Conroy easily supplies.

"If he was an underground fighter then what the hell did he need a secretary for that he ran off with?" Kayler rambles.

Great, as if I needed the reminder. Due to my petty emotions and the asshole I'm currently suturing, I might have just shoved the needle a little deeper than necessary.

Steeling my emotions, I keep my voice even when I switch to a long gash on his side to clean and close it with stitches as I recite out the facts I recently became aware of. "I just found out he owned a copy center as a coverup. Duck-face was running the shop for him and acted as his secretary to schedule appointments so they could organize the fights together. It's quite the eye opener when you've been oblivious for years until the man you thought you loved kicks you to the curb and throws years' worth of shit he thought was annoying about you right in your face. Makes you feel real damn stupid for trusting someone who doesn't so much as blink as he fucks you over."

This time the man stays silent and lets me work.

That is until he says to my sister, "We need to talk once I'm stitched up."

Olcay doesn't say a word and completely ignores him. I have no clue what the hell is going on between those two, but I can clearly see something's not right. At some point Olcay slips out of the room. Kayler finally takes notice of Olcay's absence when I'm done and tries to get up, probably to track my sister down.

I shove him back in his seat. "I'm not going to patch you back up if you rip your stitches. You're going to stay right here and rest. It'll also give you some time to think about your mouth and how you let your asshole shine right through it when you opened it. If it's not clear…don't talk to my sister that way again. I don't care whose son you are, you will get kneed in the balls. Understood?"

He doesn't say another word but his expression lets me know he's pissed off. I start to clean up and recognize a sedative and at this point I think it's best to knock the asshole out so he can give his body some rest to let it heal. The way he's pumped up I'd say he won't do it if I only tell him to take some rest.

I give him the shot and tell the biker next to him to make sure to watch over him. I'm itching to get back home to check on Baxter. A moment later Conroy is leading me back to his house. A house I just called home. Holy shit.

I just stitched up this man's son who suffered knife wounds. What the hell are we being dragged into now? Something about going from bad to worse sends a chill down my spine. I hope to hell things will settle down sooner rather than later but with my luck? I doubt it will.

CHAPTER 05

CONROY

I'm pissed off. I had little sleep and the shit that went down yesterday with my son getting stabbed resulted in me bringing home one shut-down woman. She didn't even want to discuss anything, simply excused herself and retired to her son's room.

Hence the little to fucking no sleep I had and was in my living room before the crack of dawn when I received a phone call from Sam, a friend of mine who works in law enforcement. I've asked him to keep a look out in case Detta's ex's name pops up anywhere.

Turns out...the fucker popped up; face down floating in the river along with the chick he ran off with. Well, it's safe to say the running off part didn't happen because someone caught on before they so much as had a chance to leave town and killed both of them.

Needless to say, Bo fucked up big time and I'm glad I brought Detta and Baxter to my house to give them a safe place. I have no clue if the one who killed those two is also after Detta but I'm going to find out.

It's why I'm sitting at the clubhouse in church with a full table. I've asked my son's old lady and Detta's sister to join me so we can talk a few things through. I'm doubting bringing the woman into church when my son stalks into the room and the two of them start to bicker.

I don't have time for this shit and I raise my voice to boom through the room, "Cut it the fuck out you two."

"Yes, Prez," Kayler grumbles.

I place my hands on the table and lean in to lock my eyes on Olcay when I say, "There have been some developments. Now, Olcay, I have asked you to be here with us but I demand your full honesty and loyalty. Mainly when it comes to keeping your mouth shut toward your sister."

"You have my honesty and loyalty," Olcay starts and taints her voice with firmness when she adds, "But my sister has it without even asking or demanding it from me. I will not go behind her back, nor will I do that to any of you." She pins Kayler with a harsh look. "Nor will I judge or assume without any previous communication."

"Fair enough," I rumble. "This being said, there

will be a chunk of information we won't share with you. Not because we doubt your integrity but there are things I don't want your sister to become aware of."

"Then I guess maybe it's better if we all cut ways," she snaps. "Two days ago, neither of us was aware of the other. I've spent my two silent nights here. Silent as in I was told what goes on in this place won't ever leave these walls. The money I needed for my sister to clear away the debt that wasn't even hers to begin with landed in my lap when I took the stripper job. So, we have that part handled. I'll leave you guys to it to finish your meeting while I get my sister and nephew so we can get out of your hair, life, whatever." She lets her gaze slide over the faces sitting at the table, avoiding Kayler in the process until her eyes land back on me. "Thanks, though. For everything."

I steel my voice for what I'm about to tell her, and every single one sitting at the table. "You're welcome but that's not going to happen. You two are tied to the club. You because my son claimed you, your sister because she's mine."

"Excuse me?" Olcay gasps.

"As of yesterday everything was handled and wrapped up," I grunt, ignoring the shock on her face. "With the last two idiots of Ace Blaze MC taken out we've successfully ended the threat. There's just the missing piece of information Kayler caught yesterday we need to clear up. So, mind telling us why the crates stashed at Eli's place had your address on them?"

Her eyes widen at the little piece of information I just told her. "What? How's that possible? Wait. Crates. They were delivered to the dancing studio. I have no clue where they came from or what was in them. All I know is that there were some shipment already on their way when I bought the place. I thought it was harmless." She swallows hard and croaks. "What was in those crates?"

"Guns," Kayler grunts from beside her. "Who did you buy the place from?"

"Bo Fielder," she mutters. "My sister mentioned he had the place up for sale when I was looking for a space to start my dancing studio. It was perfect since it also has an apartment above it. I…I didn't think a shipment of any kind would be weird because it made sense when Bo mentioned how it was already shipped from Europe and took time to be delivered. He wasn't planning on selling the building to me at the time of the shipment so it made sense to agree to accept the delivery for him. He told me he would send over some men to come pick it up and they did." She releases a deep sigh and rubs her temples. "I can't believe I'm this stupid. Wait. Does this mean Bo is involved with Ace Blaze? Is he a weapon dealer? Oh shit. My sister. My nephew. What did Bo pull them into? I think I'm going to be sick," she groans and closes her eyes.

They flash open when Kayler covers his hand

with hers and says, "Calm down, darlin'."

She pulls her hand from his. "Don't," she snaps. "You're an asshole. You thought I was working with Bo…with those other bikers…the one who shot at us…didn't you?"

The wince on Kayler's face betrays him but he starts to explain anyway. "I didn't know what to think with you landing on my doorstep, too good to be true, and then seeing your address on those crates… it fucked with my head. I knew there should be a logical explanation, but I jumped to conclusions. I shouldn't have. I am an asshole. I can't change that and I will fuck up some more along the road ahead of us. If anything…I think our lives crossed for a reason. For one to pull your asses out of the danger you three were unintentionally wrapped in. But mostly? For me to be knocked on my ass and be reminded of the fact that one should look at themselves first before judging others. Count to ten or to a hundred before firing off shit that runs through your head. If I would have, there wouldn't be a gaping hole of anger I'd have to cross to get you back in my arms."

"Touching. Though, those last few lines make you sound like a pussy," Binx remarks.

Olcay whips her head in his direction. "Shut up or I'll have my old man kick your ass for disrespecting him. And I don't mean about the stuff you mentioned just now, but in my opinion that's just as disrespectful."

"Binx runs on disrespectful," Kayler snarls.

"Something he's going to be buried six feet under for soon enough."

"Focus," I snap. "This bickering can be resolved later. Back to the shit at hand." I let my gaze find Olcay's. "Bo Fielder and his secretary were found floating in the river this morning. I won't be able to hold this piece of information back for your sister and the kid but I would like to firmly tell you that you should leave the connection of the crates, your address, and Bo's possible involvement with Ace Blaze a secret. I don't want her to worry about possible backlash coming from this. Mainly for the kid but she's struggling herself to keep their heads above water as it is. From what I've found out, she's been killing herself with double shifts at the hospital for months, if not years, to make ends meet while Bo was spending her money and everything the fucker made. He took everything they had to make a great escape…something we now know failed and I'm going to find out if there will be any backlash from his actions that might blow onto your sister and the kid. Get what I'm saying here?"

I can tell by the frown she's sporting she's trying to process the shit I just told her. It's a lot to take in and I've been letting this information roam around in my head ever since I received the call this morning.

Olcay bobs her head as she reaches for Kayler's hand. Things must be falling into place, especially the way my son jumped to the conclusion of her being involved since the crates were delivered to her address.

It's the reason we're having this talk because neither of us knew and now we do…Bo, that fucker, has deeper connections than we all thought.

"Odette doesn't need to know what Bo was involved in if he's dead now," Olcay eventually says. "I hope there's no backlash and appreciate you looking into it to make sure. You have my word; I won't say anything. Hell, Baxter doesn't need any of it, especially now that the little man doesn't even have a father to clean up his act because he sucked at being a dad for that boy and now he only has his mother to take care of him."

"He has me," I want to growl but I bite my tongue. She doesn't need to hear my overbearing protectiveness that's rising high and strong. From her expression I can already tell her throat is clogging up with emotions. I'm sure she's now aware of the severe risk her sister and nephew have hanging over their head.

Kayler is about to speak up but Binx beats him to it when he says, "The boy not only has his mother, he has you, and all of us as well."

Kayler grunts in agreement and glances Binx's way. "Nice save but I'm still gonna kick your ass after I hear in which way you disrespected my woman."

Binx rolls his eyes. "Whatever, dude. I know where my loyalty lies. I might dance on the borders of this brotherhood but no one but me gets to ditch other brothers, old ladies, or anyone else connected to the club, especially that little man."

Kayler and Olcay share a look before she snaps, "My old man will still kick your ass."

Binx shoots her a grin. "Looking forward to it."

I end the meeting and they all stroll out of church. The damn hard part is about to come; telling Detta and Baxter about Bo. Though, I'm first going to have a talk with Detta without the kid because she needs to be the one to tell him.

Taking my phone out of my pocket I make a quick call to my contact to ask if there are any developments in the cause of death or any other information he can give me. Sadly, there's still not much to go on and I can't prolong this any longer.

With a heavy heart, I step out of church. I scan the main room of the clubhouse to make sure Olcay is there to watch Baxter but come up empty. He must be in his room. Strolling down the hallway, I knock on the door and when he opens, I let them know what I'm about to do.

Stalking back to the main room, I come to a stop in front of Detta. "Hey. I need for you to come with me."

She glances up at me and frowns. "Why?"

My eyes slide to Baxter and back to her. "I'll let you know as soon as we're in church…alone."

She instantly gets to her feet and Olcay takes her place beside Baxter. I hold the door open for her and once inside I make sure to lock it and take a deep breath before facing her. Her arms are defensively crossed in front of her chest.

"Okay, lay it on me, what did you drag us into? I appreciated how you swooped in to save the day but it seems you guys are handling much bigger issues judging from the way I had to stitch your son up last night," she snaps.

"Kayler getting a few slices was during a clean-up action we needed to do because–"

"I don't want to hear it," she growls, cutting me off. "It's your business and not connected to me or my son. Maybe it's best if we leave. If you are still handling the loan shark this means we have the five grand we could use as a start to live somewhere else."

"Not happening," I growl, unable to catch myself.

"Not happening?" she throws back in a sarcastic voice and perches her fists on her hips.

Fuck. This is not going the way I planned. "Detta," I sigh, trying to control my frustrated anger.

"It's Odette," she firmly states. "Again, appreciate the hospitality but–"

"Could you just fucking sit down and listen to me for one goddamn minute, woman?" I growl and instantly regret it, but I can't take it back. I rub my temples with one hand and mutter, "Please, Detta. I'm trying to tell you something terrible about your…please. Just sit down and hear me out."

I drop my hand and notice she's staring at me.

All the anger and frustration have drained from her and her arms are hanging slack beside her body.

Stepping closer instead of sitting down she asks, "What's wrong? Just tell me. I don't want to sit down. When people ask others to sit down it's…shit. Somebody died. That's it, right?" Her hand flies to her heart and she fists the fabric of her shirt. "Baxter is in the other room and so is my sister. There's no one else out there I care about…oh no. It's Bo, isn't it?"

"I'm so sorry," I softly tell her.

She closes her eyes, nods, and swallows hard.

All I want to do is take her into my arms but the reaction she gave me when we stepped into church shows me her emotions are all over the place and now the news hits her about her ex, the father of her son. It's not my place to comfort her and that fucking hurts just as much as watching her process the loss of her child's father and what she's about to face; telling her son his father isn't coming back.

CHAPTER 06

DETTA

My heart is racing and my throat clogs up. Swallowing hard, I try to push my emotions down and hopefully keep my voice strong when I ask, "How?"

"I asked a friend of mine who works in law enforcement to keep an eye out in case your ex's name popped up. This morning I received a call bright and early that they found, and identified, your ex floating in the river along with a female body."

He takes a step forward at the same time I take a step back. The wince on his face is killing me. I know I lashed out a moment ago but it seems irrelevant now. I mean, my issues trump his or at least put them at the same level.

Hell, didn't he just mention Kayler was injured due to a cleanup action. Clean up means something is over because the last thing you do is clean up.

All while my issues have just started. Bo was found floating in the river, a woman as well…they killed him. Am I next? Baxter? Oh. My. God.

Without thinking I launch myself at him. He doesn't expect the move and grunts as he steps back but quickly wraps his arms around me. I bury my head into his chest and breathe him in. His spicy, manly scent calms me as I hug him tight.

I need this man. Not only because he takes action and seems to have a solution for whatever is thrown his way but mostly because he's this pillar that keeps me grounded. The moment my life went to shit there was desperation, not knowing what to do.

My sister taking a job for five grand, to do something she would never do in a million years, felt wrong but there was no other way. Then this man comes swooping in. A perfect stranger and I should hesitate or refuse but instead, through the havoc everything feels insane, as if I'm losing a grip on life itself.

Except when this man is holding me or telling me he'll handle it. Because he's kept his word so far. Offering his home to me and my son, the time and attention he gave Baxter without a complaint, being annoyed, or thought of it as a chore or a way to get in my pants.

This man is genuine. Maybe it's because he's older, more experienced; knows the crack of the whip life can lash out at any time. Everything is blurry but one thing is damn clear; Conroy is exactly what I need right now.

The dreadful and unavoidable thought enters me. "I have to tell Baxter."

His large hand cups the back of my head. His lips brush against my forehead when he whispers, "I'm right here if you need me. We can do it together, whatever or however you want to handle it."

"I…I never thought…I wished him dead so many times since he left and took everything. I…how am I?" I groan and feel hot tears sliding down my cheeks. "How can I face my son while deep down I'm glad he won't be back to hurt us? I'm a horrible, horrible person."

Conroy cups my face with both hands. "No, you fucking aren't. Those are emotions tearing through you. It's normal to hate the person who kicked you down and left you in the damn dirt. It's a human reaction, as is the way you need to muddle through the time to come to process everything, handle the grief, your son, the funeral…there's a lot to deal with but you're not alone. Your sister is right there with you and so am I, as is the rest of the brotherhood. Whatever you need."

The words "thank you" are balancing on my lips but I gave them to him so many times already. So instead, I lean forward and breathe in his strength for another few heartbeats.

I release a deep sigh. "Kids…they're innocent. They should be kept out of the shadows. Hell, they are the fucking light in our lives and it's our damn job to keep them shining bright until they're able to hold their brightness on their own. And then we're still there if the light flickers. Baxter is so young and yet he knows exactly what goes on around him. The ability to understand, process, mourn, give grief a place…it's all jumbled and so fragile."

"You're right." His words vibrate through his chest. "Everything is jumbled and fragile but it's in moments like these, when you push boundaries, is where you hold fast. You will find the strength to pull through and from the time I spent with you, I can tell you're a great mother who puts their kid first no matter what. You can definitely tell by the way Baxter reacts to you and everything around him. That's all you. And I'm sorry to say that there is no easier way than to push through this. Explaining to your kid how his father died is gonna hurt…for the both of you. Just know at some point you're going to move past it to give your feelings and emotions a place to remember, to allow it to be a part of it but not a dark cloud clinging to you. Kids are resilient. He's young. He has you, his mother."

I fist the fabric of his shirt and take another shuddering breath. At some point you're going to move past it to give your feelings and emotions a place to remember, to allow it to be a part of it but not a dark cloud clinging to you. His sentence echoes inside my head and I know he's right, but man does this suck. Stalling won't make the tragic news disappear. Conroy is right; I have to push through this.

"You'll be there?" It might be considered a question but the way I voice those words make it more of a statement.

"I never considered leaving your side," he simply says.

Tilting my head back I stare into his eyes. I cup the side of his face and croak, "I refuse to give you those two words I've been giving you in spades ever since we met. But just know I deeply appreciate you."

He wraps his fingers around my wrist and pulls my hand from his face to place a kiss on my palm. "Right back at ya, sweetheart."

"Now let's do this because I have a few more things to share and it ain't nice. I was going to keep it from you with all this shit being thrown on your path but I'm now realizing I don't want you blindsided."

"Oh, fuck," I murmur. "He was in deeper with those underground fighters wasn't he?"

"More like weapon dealing," Conroy grumbles. "There were weapons in crates delivered to the building Olcay bought from Bo. He told her they were already shipped when he sold the building to her so if they were delivered he would send someone to pick them up. Those crates were at the house of two Ace Blaze members Kayler was at to take them out. That's when he saw the address of your sister on those crates. Ace Blaze has been dealing in guns and drugs, polluting the streets, and causing people to overdose on tainted drugs. We put a stop to the MC but didn't manage to take out all of them. A few scattered but two were hardcore enough to strike back. As I said, Kayler went after them with a few brothers and managed to take them out but got sliced up."

I bob my head to process his ramblings. "As if underground fighting wasn't enough he had to add dealing in weapons and working with a damn drug dealing MC along with it. Wait. Does this mean you guys deal in guns and drugs as well?"

"We might not do everything by the book…hell, I just told you we wiped out another MC. But we don't deal in weapons or drugs. We make a good living by hiring girls to shake their tits and ass on stage. We own a strip club which will probably kill me one day. I hate doing those damn books."

The corner of my mouth twitches. "Then hire an accountant."

"I would if I wasn't so anal about doing everything myself. I don't like anyone up in my business, it's like baring your soul to another person so they can steal the light, ideas, precious cargo, whatever the fuck they like."

I pat his chest. "Then let one of those young guys you have walking in that clubhouse of yours get a crash course in accounting so he can take it over for you. Easy solution."

A slow smile slides across his face when he murmurs, "Already working up to the title of the president's old lady."

The president's old lady? I'm about to question him about his statement but he steps away from me and heads for the door.

"Come on, we can't delay the inevitable."

With the feel of steel weighing down my boots, I put one step in front of the other until I'm standing in front of Baxter.

I have no clue what to say but it's Conroy who says with a soft voice, "Hey, Champ. Mind coming with us? Your mother and I need to tell you something."

He jumps up from the couch and bobs his head enthusiastically. I hold out my hand as he does his so I can engulf it with mine. We all head back into church and close the door for the privacy we need. I can feel the burn of tears, but I try to push them away.

Baxter climbs on Conroy's seat at the head of the table. Conroy ruffles Baxter's hair.

"Looking good there, Champ," he gruffly rumbles.

I squat down in front of Baxter while Conroy is standing behind him, looking me straight in the eye to give me the much-needed support.

I fill my lungs by taking a deep breath and slowly release it. "Baxter, honey. You know daddy left, right?"

His bottom lip trembles when his tiny head bobs.

"Something happened," I croak and my throat

gets so freaking thick I cannot push out the next words.

Tears slide over my son's cheeks and I'm a complete mess. Anger overrides the emotions that block my voice.

"Daddy died, baby. He's not coming back because he can't," I firmly tell him.

He jumps off the chair and into my arms. I'm not expecting it so I fall back on my ass and hold him tight. Sobs fill the room. Mine. His. Ours. Tears fall together and we're both lost in the moment, sitting on the ground and holding each other tight.

I feel Conroy's strong hand on my shoulder, giving me a gentle squeeze. "Come on you two. How about we check on the bike, Baxter? Get our hands dirty and talk a bit? Make your mom help out?"

"Fix the bike, fix your head," Baxter croaks.

Conroy squats down to our level. "That's right, Champ. You remembered that, huh? It's what I also used to say to my son when we had stuff to deal with, process, and work through. Life comes with ups and downs and I know you're sad and mommy is too but that's good, you remember your daddy because he was yours."

Baxter holds out his tiny hand, offering it to him the way I was offering mine to my son a moment ago. My heart squeezes at the sight before me where my son seeks strength in the man who is a rock to anyone around him. Even my kid, as small he is, realizes it.

It shows I'm making the right choice to trust my gut and stay right here, taking everything Conroy has to offer. I'd be crazy not to. Especially with everything that happened and the recent developments.

I need to keep Baxter safe and the only place that can guarantee our safety right now is here with Conroy and the brotherhood.

CHAPTER 07
Two days later
CONROY

"You're shitting me?" I grunt and take off my cap to rub the back of my head before I put it back on. "That doesn't make sense at all."

I glance at my house where both Detta and Baxter are inside. Baxter fell asleep about twenty minutes before Sam, my law enforcement contact, showed up unannounced. The past two days have been hard for both Detta and Baxter, dealing with a visit to the police station, making arrangements for the funeral, the grief, it's hard on both the kid and my woman.

Both are holding strong, though. I glance at Sam who just dumped a load of information on me about Bo and the connection to the weapons that were in the crates delivered to Olcay's address and ended up with Ace Blaze.

"Wish I was, Conroy. It's a damn mess and I have

no clue who's involved or how high up it goes," Sam grumbles.

Detta strolls out with two bottles of beer in one hand, and water in the other. She gives me a small smile and I give her a grateful one as I point at the beer. Without a word, she places the beer on the table and disappears back inside.

This woman puts all the dots on the i for me. This action just shows it. Most of the time when we have women in the clubhouse, they come close to eavesdrop or butt in but Detta merely offers a beverage and quickly slinks away so she doesn't interfere.

The confrontation we had in church, two days ago, before I had a chance to tell her about Bo, was understandable. Kayler being hurt, the stuff she's wrapped in; it makes sense she wants to back away from danger with the son she has to take care of.

Sam grabs a bottle and twists off the cap. He takes a large sip and keeps the bottle in his hand when he says, "How much does she know?"

My mouth turns into a flat line, not liking where this is going. "She was only aware of the underground fighting. Had nothing to do with organizing that shit or whatever. She's a hard-working mother who busted her ass to make sure her kid had everything, and that fucker ripped her off in any way possible."

"Or he knew what was coming and tried to set up a diversion by cheating on her," Sam grunts.

"From what I've heard, not just from Odette but her sister said the same thing, Bo was a dick ever since Baxter was born. Fatherhood didn't work out the way he thought it would and the fucker basically treated the kid like shit, and that's if he was around to give his son some attention," I sneer. "It would be nice for Odette to hear the fucker might have created a diversion to keep both her and the kid out of harm's way, but you and I know damn well it would be a smokescreen full of farts."

"I feel like we're already in a smokescreen of farts," Sam says, frustration tainting his voice.

"That's why I asked if you were shitting me and the fact it doesn't make sense. At. All."

Sam bobs his head at my words. "Philip, my buddy from ATF who reached out to me, he thinks someone from his team is leaking shit to those Europeans."

The Europeans who are shipping the damn weapons and who Bo was working with. Sam just filled me in, and I still can't believe this information. While it does make sense that Bo met these fuckers during one of the underground fights he organized, it still boggles my mind how he went from organizing fights to being the link between an arms dealer and a damn MC.

I mean, that's looking for trouble if you're only one damn man. A fucking family man. Such a fuck-up.

"He needs to flush the rat so he can take out the arms dealer and end everything. Ace Blaze is dealt with so they have no way to distribute the weapons now and it all ends here. Still, them taking out Bo and his piece on the side shows he fucked up. So, what's next? I bet your ass these guys won't simply go away if they have a good thing going here."

"So...they...what?" Sam urges. "Share your thoughts, Conroy. You know how bouncing around ideas always gives me new food for thought."

I release a deep sigh. "I think they will look for a new third party to distribute. If they are already here to protect their shipment...bet they're already taking steps to forge a new connection they can depend on."

Sam doesn't look so surprised when I share my thoughts. Hell, if I would have to guess what the expression on his face means I'd say it's guilt. Why the fuck would he feel guilty?

"Spit it out, Sam," I growl and place the empty bottle of beer a little too hard on the table, making the fucker wince.

"Philip thinks the Europeans want Silver Rain MC and they will reach out sooner rather than later. Hell, I think they are already planning something because to be honest, Conroy? My visit wasn't just to share some information. I'm here because one of your girls was found murdered in the alley of your strip club. Looks like a body dump but with her background information and thrown in front of the backdoor of her place of work I'd say it's more than a message."

I grit my teeth. "Who?"

Sam takes out his notebook from his breast pocket

and flips through some pages. "Babette Peltz."

"And you couldn't mention it when you came through the door?" I shake my head. "Dammit, one of the good girls. Did you inform her mother yet? I think she lives in a retirement home."

He releases a deep sigh. "Nah, man. Her mother passed away in the hospital last night. When I got there, I was told Babette was with her when she passed. She must have been murdered right after since the coroner mentioned the time of death was somewhere around midnight."

"Fucking hell," I mutter. "I'll see if our surveillance cameras caught something."

"You have cameras up there? Not in plain sight? CSIs are still processing the scene, they didn't see any."

"Yeah, they're there," I simply say, not wanting to elaborate since it's none of his damn business. "Like I said, you'll get them as soon as I get there. I have to talk to my men first and make sure Odette is protected."

"Take your time. I'm heading back there right now." He places his empty beer bottle on the table next to mine. "If anything comes up, let me know. Otherwise, I'll talk to you later."

"Later," I grunt and watch him enter the house.

Shit. This is not good. Not good at all and I get the gut feeling Philip and Sam are right; the Europeans want to force a collaboration with us since they are down an MC. We might do illegal shit every now and then but we sure as fuck won't burn our hands on weapons or drugs for that matter.

"Everything okay?" Detta questions.

Funny. In my mind, she's always Detta. Though, when I'm talking to a complete stranger I stick to her full name. Where I wanted to keep shit from her before, I found myself sharing some of the information concerning her ex and now I'm facing the same dilemma.

For the first time in years, I feel like I'm not alone handling life but might have another shot at having a woman standing strong beside me. Both of us are in a tailspin of danger that somehow turned out to be entwined. It's as if she's meant to be mine since our lives have already crossed in many ways.

I turn to stare into her eyes when I say, "One of the girls who worked for us as a stripper was murdered around midnight and dumped in the alley behind the strip club."

"Oh no," she softly gasps and sits down next to me. "What was her name?"

"Babette. Babette Peltz."

"Oh no." This time the words are ripped from her mouth in horror.

Her reaction can only mean one thing. "You know her?"

Her hair bounces around her head. "Yes. I've known her for years. Olcay and Babette have been friends since forever. She's actually the one who gave Olcay the chance to take the job she was supposed to do. You know, dance for Kayler for two nights and earn five grand. The five grand I needed for the loan shark. Oh no. If she would have taken the job instead of Olcay she would be here… she would still be alive."

"I highly doubt that," I mutter under my breath, getting the eerie gut feeling this shit isn't a coincidence. "Doesn't matter either way. She's dead and we're all in this situation that needs to be handled. What I'm about to tell you needs to stay between us."

"You have my loyalty, Conroy. I have a gut feeling all of this is connected and I realize the safest place for me and Baxter is right beside you. Ever since he was born it's been on my shoulders to protect him. Bo never once stepped up to be a father and I shouldn't have stayed with him, but I also didn't like the thought of Baxter growing up without a father. I was already in the process of leaving Bo but…well, I guess it's exactly like you just said; it doesn't matter either way. We're in this situation that needs to be handled. I like the thought of handling it together. Whatever comes our way or how things will go in the future because leaving you isn't on the agenda."

I reach out and wrap my arm around her waist. Staring down at her, I take in her open expression. She places her hand on my chest and stares right back at me without holding back. Her eyes are dilated and showing the same interest I have reserved for her.

She doesn't know I've already claimed her in front of my brothers but it's good she's admitted to herself and to me she's mine. Catching her lips with mine, I instantly deepen the kiss. I pull her body flush against mine to brush my cock against her belly, letting her feel exactly what her words mean.

Though, it's not enough. I need her under me, my cock sliding inside her pussy to fully claim her but sadly this is not the time. Mostly, though? I'm not in a rush to fuck her. She's my old lady; we have all the time in the world.

Breaking the kiss, I gruffly tell her, "You're mine. As the president's old lady you have the loyalty of my brothers but also a responsibility against them and the club. To stand where you are will also mean I will share most club business so you're not in the dark."

She pats my chest. "With Bo I stayed in the dark, oblivious to him switching from being a fighter to arranging those underground events and reality hit too hard too fast. I had no control of the situation and it hit hard. I have no clue what I would have done if I'd known. No, I do know. I still would have left because Bo wasn't a good man, nor a good father to Baxter. You, on the other hand, have proven through actions what kind of man you are and if it's a hint of what's to come I'd sign up for that any time of day."

"It won't be easy," I warn. "This thing we're both wrapped in will bring death to our doorstep. Hell, it already has. Bo tied the MC, Ace Blaze, to the weapon dealers and we took out that damn MC. Which means the Europeans don't have anyone to transport and distribute the weapons and according to the ATF the Europeans have their eyes set on us to take over."

"Oh shit. Do you think Babette's death was a first warning to cooperate or something? To put pressure on your other business? To show what they're capable of? Or are they pissed you took out their contact? Wait. This means it was the Europeans who killed Bo?"

"Yeah," I grunt. Liking the way her mind instantly jumps in the right direction. "It's safe to say you're right about all of those things. I have to head out to the strip club and check the cameras we have set up there. They're out of sight so the authorities, or anyone else for that matter, doesn't know about them. Hopefully they caught something."

"Good. Can you get one of the brothers to watch over Baxter? Or maybe I should ask my sister, he might wake up and need me. Shit. I should stay but I want to come with you as well." She bites her bottom lip.

"I'll text Xayne to sit in the living room. Baxter got along great with him today and he did a good job earlier." I take out my phone and shoot him a message.

A few minutes later there's a soft knock on the door. I should let her stay here but on the other hand,

I know she needs the distraction as well. She's in the middle of it right along with me. Besides, this way I get to put her on the back of my bike.

And there hasn't been a woman who has had the privilege in many, many years.

CHAPTER 08

DETTA

I needed this. The wind rushing by, speeding through the darkness while the light of his bike is leading our way. The street is empty, most people are sleeping but not us. We're wide awake, our bodies flush against one another as we dominate the road.

There's no room for thinking. The vibrations of the bike underneath me, the strong man taking lead in front of me, and the rest of the world is simply flashing by. I've never been on a motorcycle and it's quite the liberating experience.

Sadly enough, our trip comes to an end when Conroy parks in front of the strip club. It's closed but there's a lot of activity in front and on the side of the building. Different law enforcement vehicles are parked alongside the street.

Sam is standing in front of the club with his

hands in his pockets when we make our way toward him. "Conroy, Odette," he grunts.

Conroy takes out his keys and opens the door. "They must have known we were closed today. Normally we would still be open around this time."

"Right," Sam grunts from behind us as we stroll inside.

Conroy hits the lights and I take in my surroundings. The place looks like a high-class strip club and I'm guessing it would seem more sensual when the light is dimmed instead of the big bright lights.

The first thing my mind comes up with is the thought it smells clean. I thought the inside of a strip club would smell like beer and…I don't know…other raunchy stuff? Hello Judy Judgement. I know, I really shouldn't judge a place I've never been before but it's also refreshing to be caught by surprise.

The dark red, velvety-looking walls, the gold chairs with mahogany tables, and huge chandeliers hanging from the ceiling. Yeah, definitely not the interior of a strip club I'd expect but then again, I've never been to one, and I'm sure liking this one.

Conroy leads us to his office and gets behind a desk. He pulls his keys from his pocket and takes out a laptop from one of the locked drawers. Firing it up, we wait for him to show us the feed of the hidden camera locked on the back entrance of the alley.

"Kayler installed it a few months ago," Conroy explains. "As a safety precaution. There are a few others in and around the building. We never check the feed unless there's something…like now. The only ones who know about them are me and my son."

"Smart," Sam only remarks.

We all watch while Conroy scans the feed for the right time when the body dump might have taken place. A few minutes pass until we see movement in the front of the alley. Two shapes are carrying something and as they come closer they become more clear.

I gasp while a shot of fear and chills hit me all at once.

"Motherfucker," Conroy snaps and grabs his phone as his eyes land on me. "Breathe, Detta. Fucking breathe. I'm sure he's okay." He jabs the screen of his phone and places it at his ear. "VP. My house right fucking now. Take a few brothers with you. Make sure Baxter is safe and hold Xayne if he's still there. Can't explain. Be right there. Okay."

"Xayne?" Sam questions.

Conroy points at the screen of the laptop. "This backstabbing fucker has been a part of my MC for almost a decade. He's also the one watching over my old lady's son."

"Fuck," Sam grunts.

I finally find my voice and point at the screen. "The other one is Edvard Havel, he's a fighter from the Czech Republic. Bo told me a few weeks ago when the man showed up at the house. Bo didn't seem too happy about it and left to take the man with him, told me he would take him down to the building they use for training."

"Not a fighter," Sam says. "Well, he might be but I've seen details for this man. The ATF has him as a prime suspect in the illegal firearms case they are building against him. They are working with Interpol to bring the network down the fucker single-handedly built out of nowhere in the past three years. And I have no damn clue why the fucker is getting his hands dirty himself."

"He must have deemed himself safe with one of my own fucking brothers having his back," Conroy hisses between his teeth.

His phone rings and with it I hold my heart, hoping it's good news and that Baxter is still safe, sleeping in his bed and Xayne has a logical explanation for dumping a freaking body along with what they just mentioned is the enemy. Wait. Is Edvard the one who killed Bo?

I'm ripped from my thoughts when Conroy curses.

"No," I gasp, knowing my worst fear just became reality. "They have him, don't they?"

"I'm going to make a few calls," Sam rumbles and pulls his phone.

"You do what you have to do but you're going to steer clear from my club and get the fuck out of my building right fucking now," Conroy snarls. "I don't want anything to happen to the kid and as of right now you're a threat. No law enforcement is coming near us. Not now when I know they're going to reach out because they took my kid for leverage."

Conroy slams the laptop shut and locks it away. He's pushing Sam out the door who is still sputtering about needing to work with ATF. My emotions are all over the place and the only thing keeping me sane right now is the fact Conroy just called my son his kid.

I'm not alone in this. Except where I am scared shitless–desperation filling me–Conroy seems pissed and ready to kill anyone in his path until he's holding my son.

He fires up his bike and warns me, "I will be safe, but I can't guarantee I'm sticking to the speed limit."

"I trust you," I fiercely tell him and get on the bike as I wrap my arms around his waist.

He peels out of the parking space and shoots through the streets like a rocket. There's no time to think as everything flashes by. It's a good thing because my emotions are a jumbled mess. My heart hurts and my eyes are burning.

Conroy roughly parks in front of his house and I'm already jumping off the bike the microsecond it comes to a stop. The door is open and Olcay is standing in the doorway. I'm rushing past her as I hear her call out my name.

It's insane but I have to see for myself. Running down the hallway, I step into the bedroom I put Baxter down to sleep in a few hours ago. The bed is empty and there's a note on the mattress. A strong arm wraps around my waist and holds me back before I can reach out to snatch up the piece of paper.

"Think before you pick up that piece of paper," Conroy rumbles beside my ear. "Sam will be here soon enough. If you want the cops to handle this they will need to process everything as evidence."

"I want him back, Conroy," I croak.

"I know, Detta, I fucking know and I want that more than anything. We can handle this two different ways. The choice is up to you. Either we handle it as club business or let the law handle it."

"I want him fucking back," I state once again, only this time my voice is eerily quiet.

I know exactly what Conroy is saying and what it entails. The situation we're in is insane and I feel like any choice I'll make can be the wrong one.

"Anyone care to tell me what the hell is going on?" Olcay snaps.

"I'd like to know as well, what the fuck happened to Baxter and Xayne?" Kayler rumbles.

The only two people who are aware of the crucial details are me and Conroy. I'm also very much aware he shared details with me that he hasn't even told his own son; his vice president. Instead, he took me with him to the strip club.

If he didn't…if I stayed at home, Baxter would still be here. Shit. Or I'd be kidnapped along with my son, who the hell knows. What I do know is that Conroy has wiped out a whole MC without law enforcement's knowledge. He's also the only one I trust.

Decision made I turn in his arms and stare into his eyes when I say, "You bring him back. I know you can."

He gives a firm nod and stalks to the bed to pick up the piece of paper.

"Contact me when you're ready, X," Conroy rumbles the message out loud before he hands it to Kayler. "I want everyone in church right fucking now. No damn excuses. Anyone who isn't present will hand in his cut."

"Got it, Prez," Kayler grunts and jogs out of the room.

"I want you two to come to the clubhouse. We'll be in church but no wandering around." Conroy's eyes find mine before they slide to Olcay.

Shit. I totally forgot. "I'll tell her as soon as you guys are in church."

Conroy steps closer and places a kiss on my temple. "Okay, darlin'." His voice is a mere whisper when he adds, "You can share some but not all details. There's a fine balance between knowledge is power and knowing too much to spike fear. Though your sister knows her fair share since she's the vice president's old lady. Now, we need to move to the clubhouse. Like I said, I'm pretty sure Sam will be here soon and I have to talk through some shit with the brothers to make a plan."

"Let's go." I spin on my heel and rush through the house.

Footsteps behind me let me know they are

following and when I step out the door it's Olcay who appears right next to me.

"What's going on, sis?" she urges.

"In a minute," I mutter. "I'll tell you as soon as they are in church and we're safely inside."

Once inside the clubhouse, it's a storm of voices and people rushing around. A few minutes later the door to church is slammed shut and an eerie quiet falls over the main room of the clubhouse. I take a seat on the couch and Olcay leaves some space between us as she sits down to face me.

"Where's Baxter?" she asks with a small voice.

"I don't know," I honestly tell her. "Olcay." I swallow hard and decide there's no other way but to straight out tell her. "Babette was murdered."

Her eyes go wide as she gasps. "What?"

"They found her body behind the strip club. It's why Conroy and I were there tonight and we asked Xayne to watch over Baxter. He's done it before and we didn't want to call you guys before we knew more details. When we got there we became aware Xayne is involved in Babette's death so Conroy called Kayler to check on Baxter."

"Did that fucker kidnap him? He's the one who killed Babette? Oh God. What's going to happen now? Oh no." She falls silent and I don't want to share her rambling thoughts but they flood my senses anyway.

Is Xayne going to kill Baxter? Did he kill him already?

I refuse to give up hope. I cannot lose my son. I won. The fierce reaction Conroy had when he realized Xayne's involvement is the reassurance action will take place right freaking now to go after my son. Where law enforcement needs to jump through hoops it's where this MC will set fire to said hoops and ride straight through it to get what they want.

The faith I have in the president of this MC will pay off, resulting in my son being returned safely in my arms. Otherwise, I won't have anything left to live for. He's my light in a life filled with so much darkness. It's only Conroy who's my beacon; my only hope.

CHAPTER 09

CONROY

"Prez, what's going to be our next step?" Binx asks after I've given them all the details.

I take a slow breath to fill my lungs. His question has been roaming around my head since the second I knew Baxter was taken.

This time the answer hits me and I know in my gut it's the right one. "We're going to pick the places we think he could use to keep Baxter in and get him back."

Everett rubs his chin. "I can only think of two places."

"Three," I snap. "And I'm pretty sure about one place but we also have to keep in mind they could be watching the clubhouse."

"Yeah," Kayler grunts. "Though, I think you're right about Xayne acting on his own. They probably approached him and somehow managed to convince him to be the middleman."

Anger hits me. "Fucking middleman? Do you think any of the brothers here would be up for a negotiation with any fucking weapon dealer or drugs dealer for that matter? If the club wants to move forward in illegal shit, it's discussed here. In. Church. Not by taking a fucking child hostage and forcing your brothers' hands to get what you want."

"Screw the asshole's reason for doing this," Reid snarls. "We're gonna focus on a plan of action to get that boy and then we'll rip the fucker apart to get answers. Wouldn't matter, though. He betrayed us. All of us. There's no coming back from that."

"Agreed," I mutter along with the rest of my brothers.

"So, the fishing cabin at the lake is one place," Everett suggests.

Kayler nods. "His parents' house. They are out of town, spending the holidays in Florida."

"We're going to check these places but I'm going to the apartment above the bar." All eyes are on me when I voice those words.

The bar owned by the club has an apartment above it some of the brothers use when they have a late shift and need to be there the next day as well, saves a trip back and forth to the clubhouse. It's not regularly occupied and we all have a key to it.

"Fuck," my son grumbles. "I think you're right. It would be hiding in plain sight. The bar is closed today and tomorrow as well."

"Screw checking the other places," Binx says. "We should hit that one full force."

I shake my head. "Not happening. I'm not risking the little dude's life. Here's what's going to happen. Ten of us are going to stay behind. We need both old ladies protected. I don't want to risk them coming to take another hostage in case we manage to free Baxter. The rest of us will ride out, and scatter in every direction in case they have eyes on the clubhouse. We go in teams so each of us knows exactly where to ride to. I'm going to the apartment above the bar. Binx, you're with me. Kayler, I want you on the cabin in case I'm wrong because that's a remote location. Reid, you're taking lead on the location of Xayne's parents' house. Observe first, make sure it's safe before you go in. If you don't trust shit or think you need backup, call it in and we'll regroup."

"I still think we should focus on the one location," my son grumbles.

I'm shaking my head once again. "There's one scared little kid involved, son. I'm not risking anything. If I'm right? And I've done this shit a lot longer than all of you. Xayne is acting alone and has him safe. I have no clue what his reasons are but a brother doesn't give up a decade's worth of loyalty for nothing. Besides. This is my old lady's kid. My kid."

The fierce protectiveness swirling in my veins makes me stare down every single one of my brothers, challenging them to defy me on this. I'll fight, bleed, willing to fucking die for each and every one of them. They know it too and at this moment all my loyalty is fixed on getting Baxter back.

He and his mother were thrown into my life unexpectedly but at a moment where I find myself wanting to add more to life than working the books and leading the MC. Working with the kid on the bike brings back memories and flames up the craving to be part of the kid's life to teach him shit the way I did with my own son.

Hell, I haven't even felt Detta wrapped around me to know I'd want it till my last dying breath. It's a connection that's thriving on more than lust and at my age, I damn well know it's something special.

"Understood, Prez," Kayler grunts with a load of respect.

I lift my chin. "Then it's settled. Weapon up and ride out. We'll keep in contact once we arrive at the locations. Make sure you're not followed and if you are? Call it in so we're aware and can give back up when needed."

I divide the rest of the men into teams and we all rise from the table and stroll out of the room. We each have our jobs to do, and I order Binx to get on his bike and wait for me since I'll be taking my truck. The rest of the men will take their bikes but I'm confident we're going to get the boy back and I want him safely in the back of the truck when we ride back to the clubhouse.

Detta rushes toward me, her head whipping into the direction of my brothers who each have their own task to handle. "What's going to happen now?"

"Now you're going to wait for me until I come back with your boy," I tell her, hoping to fuck it's not a lie I'm feeding her.

Her bottom lip trembles but that's the only outer concern she's showing. I know she must be freaking the fuck out because it takes a lot to keep my emotions in check and it's not even my son...but it sure as hell feels like it.

She grabs my sleeveless jean shirt and fists the material. "You bring him back safely. No one else. You."

I know what she's saying. We might not have been together long but we're both aware of the growing feelings between one another.

I cup the back of her head and slam my mouth over hers. Stabbing my tongue between her lips, she opens and lets me dominate her mouth. My old boy lights up with new energy, flaming hot through my veins and filling me with a new need to protect and cherish the new direction we found.

Pulling back, I vow once again, "I will bring him back. Stay put so I don't have to worry about you, okay? There will be ten of my brothers staying behind in case those fuckers come for you."

This time she only bobs her head, her eyes filled with unshed tears, letting me see a hint of the turmoil going on inside her.

"Be back soon, babe," I murmur and leave her behind as I stride out of the clubhouse.

Bikes are roaring and heading off in any direction. I jump into my truck and peel out, keeping an eye on my surroundings to see if there's suspicious activity going on that catches my attention.

I don't think I'm being followed. This confirms my suspicion when it comes to my gut feeling telling me it's Xayne acting alone. I mean, it was weird as fuck for him and that other fuck to dump Babette's body behind the strip club.

Just the two of them. All while law enforcement considers Edvard the main player. Why the fuck he would get his own hands dirty is beyond me. On the other hand…if you keep your circle small and handle shit yourself there is less of a chance of getting caught and having it done right.

Allowing for the asshole to keep out of law enforcement's hands. Not for long, though. As soon as I have my kid safe, I'm going to put all my focus on him. I have nothing to lose when my brotherhood and newfound family are complete and will work with any connection I have to bring that fucker down.

I park my truck down the road and wait for Binx to get off his bike.

"Prez, how do you want to handle it? Go in through the bar?" Binx asks.

"No, I'm going in through the roof. The window is always open and I'm hoping the fucker locked him in the main bedroom where I can get him first. Then we'll handle Xayne."

"You can't just climb up the roof, Prez. People will see and call the cops. We don't need that shit. Wait, I have an idea." He steps toward his bike and opens his saddle bags.

"Your ideas always suck," I mutter and when I see what he's pulling from his bags I grunt, "Oh, fucking hell no."

The idiot grins. "Come on, Prez. You know it won't look suspicious if you wear this."

"Santa? You want me to dress up like fucking Santa Claus when I'm going up on the damn roof? Do I even want to know why you have that shit in your saddle bag?"

Binx shrugs. "Sometimes I like to dress up for the ladies. But you? You already have the beard to match. If folks would see you up on a roof, they'd take pictures rather than call the cops. Besides, it's the roof of our bar, all logically explained if they ask questions."

I rub a hand over my face. "I can't believe this shit."

I can't believe I'm doing this, but I do shrug out of my jeans and shirt and throw the damn suit on. It's better not to raise suspicion. Christmas was a few days ago, though it could still be believable if folks look out of the window. Besides, I might need to give a spin to the situation when I find Baxter and dressing up as Santa will give a nice excuse.

"What do you need from me?" Baxter asks as I

place a backup gun in my ankle holster.

"Stay here until I signal for you to come through the bar up to the apartment." He grunts at my words and I jog down the street.

Once I come up behind the bar I take the fire escape up and have to walk over a tiny part of the roof to reach the window. Like I mentioned, the window is always open and luckily I don't have a round belly like Santa and can easily slip through.

I freeze in place and palm my gun once I'm inside and take a moment to listen. The sound of a TV is coming from downstairs. The door to this room is open and I stealthily move to the hallway.

The door of the bedroom across from this one is closed. I whip my head left and right to make sure the hallway is clear before I check the door. It's locked but the key is hanging on the wall next to it since this is a shared place.

Anyone who wants to sleep here can use that key to lock the door from the inside if they grab it. I now know I'm in the right place because this door won't be locked if the key is hanging on the wall; it would be left open to air the place.

I try to be as silent as possible when I slide the key in and unlock the door. The sight before me hits me straight in the damn chest. Baxter's panicked eyes are fixed on me as he's lying hog-tied and gagged on the damn bed.

Fucking hell.

I swear to myself right here, right fucking now;

Xayne is going to die for this. Him and that Edvard fucker who caused havoc on this little boy's life he doesn't deserve.

CHAPTER 10

CONROY

"Hey, Champ," I whisper. "I'm gonna get you out of here, okay?"

Tears are falling down his damn cheeks as his tiny head bobs. I take out my phone and shoot a quick text to my son and Binx to let them know I'm with Baxter. Shoving the thing back into my pocket, I squat down in front of Baxter.

"Okay, Champ, here's what we're gonna do. I'm going to carry you out of the building but we're going through the window and down the roof to the fire escape on the side of the building. I need you to stay as quiet as possible. Do you think you can do that for me if I remove your bindings?"

He furiously nods and I can tell by the look in his eyes he wants to be tough. Goddamn this kid.

"So proud of you, Champ," I fiercely tell him

and remove the gag. "Stay still for me, I have to cut through the tape."

He stays rock steady as I take out my knife and quickly dispose of the bindings that keep him hogtied. Who the fuck does that to a four-year-old? As soon as I've put away the knife and hold out my arms, he flings himself at me. Tiny arms wrap around my neck where he buries his head.

"I knew you'd come," he whispers. "You or Mommy."

My chest constricts and I cup the back of his head to keep him close. "I'll always come for you, Champ. Mommy wanted to come but I'd told her we guys always stick together and had to do this without her. She's waiting on you, though. Told me to make sure I was the one to bring you home safe."

"I really want to go home now," he whispers.

Another burst of pride hits me when I realize he's calling my house home.

"Okay, son, let's get you back to Mommy. We need to be as silent as we can," I tell him.

"That's why Santa let you borrow his clothes. Santa is always quiet and he was done delivering presents, wasn't he?"

This. Kid. And thank fuck for Binx's suggestion.

"Yeah, Champ," I whisper back. "Okay, time to be Santa's helpers and do a quick, silent escape the way he does after leaving presents, huh?"

Baxter pulls his head back and brings his hand to his mouth, letting me know he's locking it and shoves the imaginary key into his pajama pocket. I bring him closer to my chest and check the hallway before sneaking stealthily out of the room and into the other. I let Baxter stand by the window before I go through it, bending over to grab the little man and easily lift him out.

"I need you to hold tight," I warn.

His arms tighten around my neck and I might regret my own words because it takes effort to take my next breath. Though, I'd rather have him holding tight so I can use my arms if need be. Luckily, I'm able to cross the roof to the fire escape and from there it's a few stairs down.

Binx is waiting for me at the end of the fire escape. "I damn well love it when your instincts are right, Prez. Thank fuck that went smooth."

"Watch your mouth when the kid's around," I mutter, but can't help but smile to know I have Baxter in my arms. Anger downs the smile quick enough when I let him know, "He had him hog-tied and gagged."

"Motherfucker," Binx growls under his breath. "What do you want to do now, Prez?"

"Now we go back to the truck and make sure Champ here is safely inside. I'm hoping VP and the rest of the guys will be here soon. Then we go back to take that asshole with us."

We jog back to the truck where I place Baxter in the backseat and change into my own clothes. A few minutes later the rest of the brothers join us.

"I want a brother behind the wheel, ready to speed off to the clubhouse in case something happens, and two on each side to keep an eye out," I order.

Kayler points at five brothers and they each slide in place in and around the truck.

I open the back door and brush a hand over Baxter's head. He's lying in the backseat. "Hey, Champ. I'm gonna be right back, okay? Then we're gonna leave straight for your mother."

"Okay," he whispers.

Leaning in I place a kiss on the top of his head and murmur, "So fierce and strong, proud of you, kid."

I quickly close the door, feeling my emotions clog my throat while I need to focus.

"Let's go," I grunt and jog in the direction of the bar.

This time we're going in through the back entrance of the bar. There's a door leading up to the apartment and I'm the one taking lead.

Weapon drawn, I bellow, "Xayne. I believe you left a note for me to find. Something about contacting you when I'm ready. Well, I'm fucking ready now, asshole."

Stepping into the room, I come face-to-face with Xayne.

His gun is aimed right at me, face paling at the sight before him when my brothers file out behind me. Brothers who stood fucking by him at one point as well but now there's nothing left for him. It's as if suddenly a realization hits him and it's damn weird.

"The kid is okay. He's upstairs. I just needed to make sure I had your attention for a proposition that benefits all of us."

"Propositions are made at the table. In church. They are not made by kidnapping kids who have nothing to do with weapon dealers. That's what this is about, right? Or is it about Babette's murder? You know, one of the best performers in our strip club. The one whose body you dropped on the doorstep with Edvard's help." If possible, the last details I just threw at him make him pale some more.

"It's not…you don't understand…it's–"

"You're right," I snap, cutting him off. "I don't understand how someone can be loyal for over a decade and then suddenly turn your back on the brotherhood."

I take a step closer and the guy aims his gun toward the ceiling. "Don't move a damn inch. I can kill the boy from right here. He's on the bed in the room above us. If I fire, he's dead."

Anger hits me hard, even if I know Baxter is nowhere near the building.

"You seriously don't want to go there," I threaten in a deadly tone and spit at his feet. "You're already a dead man for taking the son of my old lady. Fucking hog-tied him and gagged an innocent four-year-old boy who was scared to death all by himself."

Xayne's eyes widen and fill with fear.

"That's right, fucker. Be afraid. Be very fucking afraid," I snap. "Because you can shoot all you want but you're going to die either way. There will be no collaboration with the Europeans, nor will we negotiate with a fucking traitor, especially one who drags innocent kids into a war they should not be in the middle of."

He moves so damn fast, I'm almost too late to prevent him from putting a bullet in his head, causing the gun to go off and blasting half his face off. He crumbles to the floor and is barely alive as he groans and worms around.

"What the fuck?" I bellow and kick the dying man in the gut. "Tell me why, asshole. Tell me what was worth betraying us for. Betraying yourself for."

"I was…I was gonna…Europe. Surgery. Tumor. Edvard promised to…money. I have a rare…" His eyes roll back into his head and his whole body goes slack.

Disgust fills me.

"What a selfish fuck," my son growls from beside me. "If he would have brought it to the table we could have come up with a plan to see what we could do. Now…he just…what a selfish fuck," he repeats once again, voicing my exact same thoughts.

Fucking us all over because he didn't think we could cough up the money or support him if he wanted, needed, or whatever for the tumor he had. He didn't even so much as bring it to the table or share it with any of us. We had no damn idea. How's that for loyalty and brotherhood for a fucking decade? Motherfucker what an idiot.

I take my phone out of my pocket. "I should call Sam."

Kayler squeezes my shoulder. "I'll handle it. You take the kid home, Dad."

I tuck away my gun and phone and grab my son's leather jacket to pull him into a hug and give him the words, "thanks, son," loaded with emotion.

"Don't mention it. That kid's life will take a turn now that he's part of our family," he croaks.

"This shit ain't over yet but you tell Sam we will work with them to bring those Europeans down now that we have the kid safe, okay?" I tell him. "We don't want the eyes of ATF and fuck knows what law enforcement department are on their ass, landing on us as well."

"On it, Prez," my VP tells me, all business now.

I left my chin and head out the door. Jogging down the street, I come to a stop near the truck.

"Two of you follow me on your bike, the rest of you can either join your VP who is going to wait for Sam to show up, or come with us back to the clubhouse."

They all head for their bikes and I jump into the truck. Glancing over my shoulder I notice the little man is sleeping. Poor thing must finally feel safe enough and probably crashed due to the turmoil of events.

It takes a few minutes to get to the clubhouse and

I park right in front of it. Jumping out, I gently open the back door and scoop Baxter into my arms. He stirs and his eyes open to land on me. I get a crooked smile as he wraps his arms around my neck. Fuck. That feels so damn good to just see the little man smile and hold me tight.

I step inside the clubhouse, my eyes instantly connect with Detta's. She shoots out of the chair she's sitting on and crosses the distance in the blink of an eye. I pass him to her and have to wrap my arms around the both of them to keep her steady on her feet.

Sobs fill the room and I feel my own throat clog up as well. Damn it's liberating to know my feelings for these two are valid and whole. I guide Detta to the couch where she gently sits down to pull Baxter onto her lap, rocking him back and forth.

Her eyes find mine over the top of his head. "You did it. You said you would, and you did."

I place one hand on Baxter's head and with the other, I cup the side of her face. "Always," I vow.

She leans into my touch and closes her eyes, tears slipping over her cheeks. "Thank you."

Baxter murmurs something and Detta's eyes fly open. "What was that, sweetheart?"

"Conroy borrowed Santa's suit. We were Santa's helpers and climbed the roof, just like Santa."

"What?" Detta squeaks. "You climbed over a roof?"

I release an awkward chuckle. "Yeah, I think it's

best we keep the details between us, Champ. I don't think Mommy's too fond about hearing how I saved you wearing a Santa suit."

I wince while Detta's mouth twitches. "Santa's suit, huh?"

She takes her bottom lip between her teeth and I shake my head. "Binx's idea but it worked, let's keep it at that."

"Let's," she agrees, and I'm loving the hint of a smile on her face, even if it's with tear-streaked cheeks and red, puffy eyes.

Having Baxter safely in her arms, inside the clubhouse, puts my heart at ease. Now, all there is left to do is make sure it stays that way. Meaning we have another challenge ahead of us because the Europeans are still out there, and will try another way to force us into something we don't want anything to do with.

But for now, at this moment, I'm taking this as a win. Even if we lost someone we thought was our friend, our brother, who in the end turned out to be anything but. Another loss we take but I swear it'll be the final one added to the body count.

CHAPTER 11
A few days later
DETTA

That smile. I love seeing it light up his whole face as he rides the mini bike across the backyard. It took hours on end for the two of them to fix the bike enough to run and then followed the hours and days to teach him how to ride. He's steady and by himself for the first time and I couldn't be prouder.

Clapping my hands, I cheer him on as he rides past me and I scream, "Yayyyyy, way to go, Baxter! So proud of you!"

He shoots me a grin but keeps his focus on riding the bike, exactly as Conroy taught him. "No distractions; eyes on the road at all times," the man kept repeating as he kept himself glued to my son's side.

I have no clue what went on between them when Conroy saved him a few days ago but it brought them closer. I also strongly believed it helped Baxter process the traumatic event along with the time Conroy spent with him over the days.

Again, so proud of him for the way he handles everything at his young age. Maybe it's due to his age, and the overwhelming attention he gets from all the brothers, that makes him more at ease with the things that happened along with the loss of his father.

The Europeans still need to be handled and I know it's only a matter of time before we are hit with danger. It's as if there's a thunder cloud right above our heads, ready to strike at any time. It sure feels that way.

I wish those dark clouds would magically clear up. I was so scared for his life and the trauma it might have given him, also being kidnapped right after his father's death. At least the smile my son is sporting is one less thing to worry about.

"He's great with him," Olcay says from my left.

I don't take my eyes off my son and tell her with a smile in my voice, "Yeah, he is. They both love to spend time together."

"I can speak from experience…it's awesome," Kayler says as he comes to a stop on my other side and adds in a loving whisper, "He's an awesome dad."

"Yeah," I croak. "Baxter is lucky to have such an amazing role model and a friend in his life. And so am I."

I stare at Conroy who is giving Baxter some

more tips when Olcay bumps her shoulder against mine. "Why don't you ask Conroy if he joins you for a drink? Kayler and I will keep an eye on Baxter, right Kayler?"

"Hell, yes. I'm gonna take over teaching him how to ride. I know a few tricks I did when I was his age." Kayler rubs his hands together and doesn't even wait for me to give an answer but he jogs off in the direction of his father.

"Eager much," I mutter.

Olcay laughs. "Boys and their toys."

I can't help but shoot her a grin, knowing she's right. We're in the backyard of a clubhouse and these guys all love their bikes. A few days ago I saw my future crumble to the ground while now I have a vision of my son passing his driver's test knowing he would want to own his own bike one day.

"Hey," Conroy quips as he comes to a stop in front of me. "Kayler said you wanted to talk to me?"

There's a serious look on his face and I try to keep mine void of emotions as excitement spikes my veins. We have spent multiple nights together in one bed, crashing to sleep the second our heads hit the pillow.

Here and there we've had some heated kisses but nothing more. I feel as if we have managed to build a solid foundation in the time we've been together and through all the havoc life has thrown at our feet.

It has shown me how persistent, caring, and dependable this man is and I'm ready to take what we have to the next level. I crave it; I crave him. Not giving him a reply, I simply wave goodbye to Baxter and lace my fingers with Conroy's.

When we take a step in the direction of his house, which I now consider ours, I feel Conroy squeeze our joined hands. "You gonna have your way with me, aren't you?"

I don't trust my voice so in return I only give his hand a squeeze. Once inside the house, I turn to kiss him but I find myself swooped off my feet and my back plastered against the door with my next breath.

His forehead is resting against mine while his body is caging me in. "I finally get to have you. Feels like years of waiting, and anticipating, has finally granted us a moment to hit pause on life and experience time where the world solely spins due to the two of us. You have no clue how hard I've been for you. Even through the shitty things you bring the heat to warm my day. The kid might be brightness in darkness but you, Detta, you bring the heat to drive the chill from my bones."

He captures my lips with his and with it drives away the chill in my bones, filling my whole body with heat. The lust hitting me has intensified compared to the first time I met this man. I was ready to jump his bones back then but now I'm pretty sure I won't survive if I don't feel him inside me soon.

I want it. Need it. Pleasure. Bliss. This man has the ability to set my world aflame and rebuild it from the ground up. My fingers slide to his neck and I grab his baseball cap, flinging it away to let my nails scrape his scalp.

He moans into my mouth and grinds his hard length against me. My breath catches from the feel of the size of him. His hands move to my ass, kneading as he steps back from the door and starts to walk.

He doesn't break the kiss but easily finds the bedroom where he gently places me on the bed. His fingers go to his leather cut, shrugging it off and throwing it onto a chair. His white tank follows, showing me his lean body.

He slowly unbuckles and slides off the belt to throw it on the bed. "Might need that later," he grunts and continues stripping away his clothes. "Get naked, Detta. I want my mouth on your pussy so strip and spread those legs for me."

I swear my panties are drenched as soon as his last sentence hits my ears. This man. He completely has me in all ways. Not only me but my son as well. He's unique in a way I've never experienced and maybe it's because he has years of life experience added in comparison to mine but who fucking cares.

It's a feeling, an experience, actions shown how well a person matches you in all ways and that's without the physical part. That's what comes next. And holy freaking shit. He's packing some serious dick.

My heart skips a beat when he palms himself and lazily sweeps his thumb across the slit to catch the drop of precum seeping out. I'm finally naked when he steps closer to the bed and cups the side of my face. His thumb with the precum traces my bottom lip and I keep our eyes locked when I let my tongue sneak out to lick my lip and his thumb.

He groans and rumbles, "Can't wait to have you suck me off. Won't be this time, though. I have to taste you and then fuck you hard. Claim you inside out with my cum and then…then we'll catch our breath and for round two we'll start with you riding my face while sucking me off. Yeah. I like the sound of that."

His hand wraps around my throat but it's in no way painful as he guides me to my back on the mattress. He places a kiss on my sternum, catching my nipple with my next breath. A moan slips over my lips as he slowly makes his way down my body by trailing a path of kisses.

I feel him everywhere. Body. Mind. And even soul deep as he buries his face between my legs. I'm overwhelmed by this man in an utterly worshipping way. His tongue slides through the lips of my pussy, catching my clit and flicking the bundle of nerves, expertly as if he knows where the orgasms have been hiding all my life.

One slams into me out of nowhere, bliss flows through my veins as I gasp for my next breath. Both my hands fly out to keep his head in place as I shamelessly ride his face to prolong my pleasure.

His rumble of approval ripples through me. He places a soft kiss on my mound as he climbs up my body. I can feel the hot tip of his dick brush my entrance, effortlessly finding its home as he thrusts forward.

His mouth is close to my ear, his breath as hot as his words when he rumbles, "Gonna fuck you now," as he slams his hips forward, filling me completely with one stroke.

"Conroyyyyy," I moan and wrap my legs around his hips as he indeed starts to fuck me.

I gladly surrender to the rough and overwhelming way he dominates my body. Where I had just come down from a ride of bliss, I can already feel the spark of another orgasm lying right around the corner.

This man is the complete package, one I know I've been waiting all my life for but rarely enough has to come at the right time at the right moment. Our moment is clearly now where the both of us are at a point in life where we're open to a new start, a new future, a new beginning.

My orgasm takes me once again by surprise and I dig my nails into his back to keep him close as my pussy ripples around his dick.

"Fuuuuck, yes, woman. You feel good. Damn good. But I'm not done with you yet," he grits through his teeth as if he's in pain.

I'm barely recovered from my second orgasm when he suddenly pulls out and flips me over, positioning me on my knees. He takes the belt and catches my hand, taking the other one and binds both my hands together. He now has both my arms pinned on my back, gripping them with one hand as I feel him guiding his dick to my pussy, slowly sliding back inside me.

One hand is on my shoulder, the other on the belt around my wrists as he takes me from behind, easily controlling my body. Electricity zings through me each time he roughly fills me up. I've never been taken this way and I'm loving it.

The stamina, dominance, grunts ripping from him, the slapping of our bodies, everything cocoons our desire and lust for one another as pleasure once again boils over inside me. Only this time I feel him thicken inside me as his cum sates my orgasm until I'm crashing face forward into the mattress, completely spent.

I'm vaguely aware of how Conroy gently takes off the belt and throws it onto the floor. He pulls me close as he spoons my body. I sigh in complete contentment. At this moment, there are no worries eating at my thoughts, only the post-orgasm fog my mind is still wrapped in.

"I adore this…you," I blurt and suck in a breath, shocked I blurted out my thoughts without thinking things through.

Conroy doesn't seem to mind or catch my moment of non-filter when he says, "I've adored the fuck out of you ever since you opened the door for me with that mouth filled with sass."

"I wish my heart was devoid of fear because I

only want it filled with the moments I experienced today. The joy on Baxter's face and yours, followed by the bliss we created together. I want this life with you and my son along with all the other brothers in this MC who are caring and helpful. It's rare…family…so perfect." I bite my bottom lip to keep from rambling.

His arm tightens around me. "Same here, babe. Same here. And we'll have that, soon." He chuckles and adds, "Sam and Philip are waiting at the clubhouse. I should have been in a meeting with them twenty minutes ago."

"What?" I gasp and jolt up to turn and face him. "You have that ATF agent and Sam waiting for you? Why are you cuddling with me?"

He places a kiss on my nose. "Priorities. That's why. But since you're up instead of a boneless heap in my arms we might as well head over and see what they have to say."

I swing my legs off the mattress and turn to face him, not caring at all that I'm still fully naked, his cum sliding down my legs. Ugh. Yikes. Bathroom break before getting dressed for sure.

Though, I do have to ask, "We? As in you're going to allow me to sit in during the meeting?"

He grabs his jeans and pulls them on. No underwear. Huh. Sexy. Dammit, focus.

"Yeah, Detta. You're the president's old lady and just as deep in this shit as I am. There are no secrets and we sure as hell ain't going to work with the

Europeans so we need to end this by working together."

"Thank you," I honestly tell him. "For everything and I know I keep saying it but you're a true gem, treating me like an equal in every way."

He closes the distance and wraps his arm around my waist and kisses me hard.

Pulling back, he slaps my ass. "Get cleaned up and dressed, we have club business to handle."

I grin up at my old man. "Yeah, we do," I tell him, feeling as if we're an invincible team, as I dash into the bathroom.

CHAPTER 12

CONROY

I feel like I'm on top of the world. Shit be damned if there's still a risk of the Europeans wanting to force us into their weapon business. We'll fight tooth and nail, especially now that I have everything I wanted.

Complete. I feel utterly complete with Detta and Baxter entering my life and filling the hole that was left behind when I became a widower. I already knew she'd be right for me when I first laid eyes on her. The kid and I got along but with what we finally had a chance to do just now? It certainly sealed the deal.

The way she's glowing I'd say the feeling is mutual. It's also the reason why I'm taking her to the meeting. She has just as much a clear vote in how this shit is handled as me. It's not just me, her, and the club's safety; it's her kid's as well. His life was put on the line more than once so she gets to have her voice heard in this, I'll make sure.

Besides, she's already shown me she can handle different situations and knows very well when to keep her lips sealed or when to speak up if needed. She's the president's old lady through blood and bones.

"Sam," I grunt as we walk into the main room of the clubhouse.

He takes my hand and gives it a firm squeeze. "Conroy. This here is Philip Deckers, ATF."

I grunt and shake the man's hand. "Conroy Lears. This here is my old lady, Odette Jarsdel." I don't let the fucker give her a hand but point at church and tell them, "Let's take this conversation somewhere more private."

We all take a seat and Philip speaks first. "We've been working with Interpol and have managed to map out the people working with Edvard Havel. The only thing we haven't been able to do is track down the man himself. As soon as we have a location on him we will all work together to bring them down simultaneously."

"And you're here because?" I impatiently snap, knowing what's coming but hope to fuck I'm wrong.

"We need your help," Sam says, confirming my suspicions when his eyes land on Odette.

"No," I grit. "Not just no, but hell the fuck no. You want my old lady to reach out to him, right? Put her in the spotlight to draw him out?" I shake my head. "Not going to happen. My woman and her son have been in the middle, at risk, for far too long. I won't have it. Baxter was lying hog-tied and gagged on a bed by one of my fucking own due to that fucker and you want his mother's help so he'll risk losing her as well as her father? Not happening."

"I don't think either of them poses a threat to Edvard," Philip says as his gaze finds mine. "If anything, I'd say they are quite safe, especially the kid."

I narrow my eyes. "And why is that?"

His attention slides to Detta. "Bo Fielder, your ex, was one of Edvard's half-brothers. His other half-brother is still in the Czech Republic, running things from there. Another one is working in the harbor and we were able to make a link due to the information on when the crates were shipped to your sister. We believe they want you and the kid. They probably killed Babette Peltz because she interfered, making you and your sister move into the protection this MC offers."

"Holy shit," Detta murmurs.

"We have a good chance to catch them all if you are willing to help draw him out. Edvard is considered the head of this family business. If we bring him in and have other teams working around the world to arrest the others simultaneously, we will be able to wipe them out completely," Sam urges.

I'm not liking the sound of this at all. The round 'em all up at once does, but the rest of this story doesn't add up. "Why would Edvard kill his own half-brother if they have a good system going for them as you said?"

Philip winces and I'm guessing this is the part he would rather have kept from us. But then his eyes shift to Detta and I regret asking.

Even more when Philip says, "We've heard from a few fighters we arrested that the man hated his family. He wanted to be in charge and expand the underground fighting, ditching the weapon deals he needed to handle for his half-brother. His kid and wife kept him rooted in this town while he wanted to switch states to start over. He saved up money from fights, and the weapon transfer, cleaned out the shared accounts, and didn't pay anything to get as much cash as he could to start over somewhere new. He didn't count on word spreading to his half-brother, and for sure didn't think Edvard would cross the ocean to take charge of the situation. Not to mention, killing him for his betrayal."

I process his words but they still don't sit well with me. Especially the part where, "If you say Edvard killed his own half-brother for his betrayal, why would my woman and Baxter be safe from his wrath?"

"Our sources say Edvard wants both the woman and the kid," Philip states. "An instant family, something he has been unable to have. Rumors say he's unable to reproduce."

"You gotta be fucking kidding me." I rub a hand over my face. "For the record? You're insane if you think that'll make it safe for them to be near him. It's twisted. You can't force a woman or a kid to become an instant family. Hell, putting a kid in this world doesn't make you a damn father or a mother, it's the everyday actions that make you live up to become a damn parent."

Detta reaches out and places her hand on my forearm. The smile tugging her lips warms my chest exactly the way adoration shines from her eyes.

Her head turns and she stares Philip down. "What exactly are you asking of me?"

I'm damn proud of my old lady, not beating around the bush but demanding for them to be clear about what the hell they came here for.

"We know there's an office somewhere in town where a handful of trainers would meet with Bo to set up the location of the next fight and such. None of the fighters we talked to know about this location and there aren't any businesses linked to him by name. You would think he'd ditch that office as well but he wanted to continue the underground fighting, the meeting place would have been the only thing solid." Philip glances at Sam. "We think Edvard would be staying there if he was the one paying for this location so it wouldn't have been tied to Bo but to Edvard."

Detta frowns. "I really have no clue. I only went with him to the fights when he was still fighting himself. That was years ago. I didn't like it one damn bit but I do dare say that when I first met Bo I was enthralled by the whole bad boy vibe of it. But it gets old really fast especially since I'm an ER nurse. Meaning I don't like stitching up people who get hurt at their own expense and for the entertainment of others. Especially after I gave birth to Baxter. That's also when the friction between us started and went from bad to worse. I've told you I only saw Edvard once. Bo left with him instantly and only mentioned he'll take him to the candy store. It's an old building where he used to train and worked out with other fighters."

Philip and Sam share a look and it's Sam who asks, "What's the address?"

"Second street, the corner of main. It's a worn-out pink building," Detta informs them.

"That part of town is locked tight and you will see vehicles coming from a mile away, probably why they used it as a meeting ground." Philip locks eyes with me. "Would you be willing to check it out for us? Edvard won't make a run for it if he spots you there. If an unmarked police car drives through he might spot it. We need to make sure he's there so we can plan the international arrests at the same time so they won't have a chance to warn one another."

Detta squeezes my arm where her hand is still warming my skin. "We'll do it."

I narrow my eyes at her. "He asked me to ride by the address, I'm not risking your ass."

"I'll be safe on the back of your bike and like you said, we'll only ride by the address. Don't you think we have a better chance to draw him out if he sees me? We haven't left the clubhouse since Baxter was kidnapped. Maybe this is exactly what we need to do to make sure they can catch all of them. It could all be over by the end of the day." Her pleasing eyes are killing me.

"Life is rarely flowing in the direction you're mapping out inside your head, darlin'. You of all people should know." I release a deep sigh. "But I do understand the need to do this." I glare at Sam and Philip. "You better not be fucking with us. If something does happen–"

"It won't," Philip grunts, cutting me off. "We'll be right around the corner in a van. We will have a team on standby so we can take action within minutes."

"A lot of fucking shit can go wrong within minutes," I grumble. "Fine. Let's do this. Give me a moment to let my VP know what we're about to do so they can be on standby as well."

I stalk out of church and shoot my son a message. A moment later he strolls into the main room of the clubhouse. I quickly give him an update and he also speaks up with his concerns but I'm backing up my old lady on this. Besides, if we can end it today it would mean we can start off the new year without any concerns.

It takes another thirty minutes for Philip and Sam to make sure there's a team in place. I fire up my bike and take my time to get to the address. The only thing soothing my restlessness is my woman's arms wrapped tight around me.

Once I ride into the street, I hear Philip's voice in the earpiece he handed me earlier. "Stop in front of the building and don't get off the bike. We want to draw him out not have the two of you disappear in the building."

I don't bother replying but I slightly turn back to tell Detta, "Keep your ass on the bike or I will make sure my handprint will decorate it for a long damn time."

Her gorgeous eyes lock with mine. "I'm betting your handprint is still on my ass from the way you smacked it earlier today. So, you might think again about making a threat because that one doesn't impress me much."

A bark of laughter rips from me. "Fuck, woman. You're really something."

"You two are hard to arrange a meeting with," a voice rumbles from my left.

Fuck. Talk about a bad moment to get distracted.

"Edvard," I grunt, hoping Philip orders his team to jump into action.

"Conroy," the man fires back. "Mind coming inside so we can have a profitable discussion? I have an offer I'm sure you won't be able to deny. Odette, you too."

I'm already shaking my head. "Afraid not. We were just passing through. I promised to take my old lady out for some coffee."

Edvard's hand moves under his jacket and I catch

a glimpse of a gun. "I'm sorry but I must insist."

From the corner of my eye, I notice movement by men in black. If Edvard sees them he'll start shooting. The fucker doesn't even care about his own blood and will only save his own ass, shooting at anything to get away.

Everything goes to shit as soon as that thought crosses my mind. Edvard indeed catches the movement and whips out his gun, ready to aim it at my woman. I lunge at Edvard before the gun heads in her direction.

Faintly I hear the bike crash when my fingers wrap around his wrist. I can't worry about Detta getting hurt because of it; I need to keep her safe from bullets rather than scratches. The fucker tries to kick me in the balls and I manage to elbow him in the face. Weight slams into us and we all crash to the ground.

There's a turmoil of black-covered arms and then I'm being pressed with my face into the pavement, my arms locked behind my back and a knee between my shoulder blades. Detta is screaming at them to let me go.

Finally, Philip's order flows through the air and I'm being lifted off the pavement and the zip tie is cut from my wrists.

"Fucking hell, so much for shit going easy," I grumble and rub my wrist but have to catch my woman when she launches herself at me.

"You saved me," she murmurs.

I stare down at her and brush my lips against her forehead. "Always and anytime, darlin'. You're not getting rid of me. You and Baxter are mine."

Her eyes fill with unshed tears, pure happiness twinkling in her eyes when she says, "We're yours. Always and anytime."

The most perfect thing I've heard in a long damn time. Nearly as perfect as knowing this might have gone wrong in so many ways but instead shit went right for once. Especially when Philip lets us know later that day that the international arrests went flawless as well.

Finally, we can put all of this behind us and focus on what matters most; family, loyalty, and brotherhood. All the love that's left in these old bones belongs to the woman who sparks youth in my heart, jolting the need to live life to the fullest. With her by my side and Baxter to add to the challenge, I have more than I could ever wish for.

EPILOGUE
Five years later

DETTA

"It's not Christmas anymore, he's almost ten years old, doesn't believe in Santa, and still demands your man to dress up like Santa. Not to mention, demands for mine to join in while wearing an oversized one himself." Olcay grins and I can't help but smile when I turn my head her way.

It's the day after Christmas and Olcay's right, it's become a bit of a tradition for the guys to dress up in a Santa suit. Baxter created the tradition by asking Conroy to put on a Santa suit along with him one year after he was kidnapped. Something about them being Santa's helpers.

How can I be against something that helped him put something negative into a positive, family thing? He never mentioned the kidnapped part, only Conroy saving him and how they had to go over a roof and down the fire escape.

Excitement is still vivid in his voice when he tells the story. Over the years he's hyped it up but I guess it's better than him remembering those days of being a train of tragedy. His biological father does have a place in his past but if you ask anyone, they'd tell you Conroy is his father in every sense of the word.

Baxter started calling him Prez the way Kayler says it and to me, they sometimes make the word sound exactly the same as Dad. It warms my heart the way we've all grown into a tight family over the years.

That reminds me. "Are you telling me you and Kayler skip the whole strip and shake your ass tradition? You know, the reason why the both of us landed our asses in this MC?"

My sister's head tips back, and a bark of laughter rips from her. "Hell yes. Each and every year I still manage to surprise him. Of course, he expects it but doesn't know when or where and that's the angle of excitement that keeps the tradition fun."

I glance at Conroy and know exactly what she means. We might not have the same tradition but we sure keep the excitement in our relationship. He's become such a rock in my life from the day I met him and he's stayed that way ever since.

He's supportive when it comes to my job. I did cut back my hours, opening up to my new life where I didn't feel the pressure of making sure there was enough money, health insurance, and all the other important things because Conroy did his part in our strong bond.

It's quite the difference and noticeable if you've been in a relationship where everything always landed on my shoulders. It's a stark reminder never to take anything for granted and to step up for what I deem important.

And I did make a promise to myself never to settle for anything less but with Conroy there's nothing to complain about. There's a balance we've found that works perfectly for us. This might sound like a fairytale and a perfect dream but life never is.

I support him in every way when it comes to being the president of a motorcycle club and it's not always easy. As is his support when it comes to my job, my sass, or Baxter for that matter. The boy is on a fast track to becoming a teenager and I think he might just like finding the rebel inside him.

Luckily enough there's a whole clubhouse filled with testosterone who all step up and are there for one another. It's one of the most important things in this brotherhood. Even if we were confronted with betrayal it doesn't mean it leaves a stain on this club. If anything the brotherhood grew stronger.

Olcay bumps my shoulder. "The way you are staring at your man I'd say you're ready to drag that Santa away to ride him all the way to the North Pole. Or ride the pole that he's hiding down south, whatever."

I gasp and spin to give her a playful shove. "Oh

stop it. And you're the one to talk when you're wearing a skimpy Santa suit for your man this time of year."

"I can lend it to you," she says and shoots me a wink.

My mouth twitches with amusement when I jerk my chin in Conroy's direction. "I think one of us wearing a costume is Christmassy enough. Need I remind you it's not even Christmas anymore."

Olcay shrugs. "Whatever. Go on, drag him off. It will give Kayler and I a chance to spend some time with my nephew. I plan on making him some Santa pancakes in the morning. Another tradition we keep in place."

"This family is full of traditions," I murmur.

"You bet," Olcay repeats.

I throw my arms around her and give her a hug. "Love you so much, sis."

"Right back at ya, sis," she murmurs and gives me another squeeze before we break apart.

Conroy's eyes land on me and I tilt my head in the direction of the door. As always the man understands me without wasting one word.

"Are they kidnapping our kid again?" Conroy quips as soon as he guides me out of the main room of the clubhouse.

"I'm not complaining," I reply.

He's right, my sister loves spending time with Baxter, just as much as he enjoys spending time with her and Kayler. It also gives Conroy and I the time to focus just on the two of us. Just as important as spending time with the three of us.

I'm so focused on getting home that I'm taken by surprise when Conroy suddenly grabs and lifts me off my feet to pull me into his office. Flipping the lock after he closes the door he instantly guides me toward the desk where he comes to a stop in front of his leather chair.

The man doesn't waste time; he never does.

Jerking the Santa pants down to his ankles, he takes a seat in his chair and rumbles, "Want your tight pussy wrapped around my cock. Fuck until we both explode."

I barely resist blurting the words, "You don't have to tell me twice." Instead, I make quick work to get naked and straddle him. Towering over my man, I stare down at him and let my fingers slide along his beard.

"I love you," I whisper while I sink down and take him inside me.

He groans and his hands grip my hips to keep me rooted to him. "You fill my life the way my cock perfectly fills you up."

"And they say romance is dead." I snort and instantly gasp when he smacks my ass.

"Fuck romance. Making sure the both of us feel right and live the way we want to, taking our kids along for the ride to show them what life is all about is what's important." He lifts me up and down his dick when he adds, "And loving you is as easy as taking one breath after another. It doesn't require thinking, it's as natural as the sun rising and falling one day to the next."

This man. Starting with the words "fuck romance," and then giving me those words right after. Instead of giving him words, I catch his mouth with mine and let him taste my emotions on my tongue.

We moan simultaneously as I start to ride him with his help. His tight grip on my hips as he guides me up and down, the way his hips shoot off the chair to fill me with force, everything heightens our pleasure.

His fingers dig into my skin, our kiss turns sloppy but the heat in our veins intensifies. I can feel him thicken inside me at the same time bliss slams into me. He grunts as his hips shoot off the chair once, twice, a final time as he comes inside me with a long groan.

I let myself crash against his chest and bury my head into the crook of his neck. Each breath I take is filled with his scent. Contentment fills me to be in his arms; right where I belong. His arms tighten around me and I feel his lips against the side of my head.

"I love you, darlin'," he rumbles.

A giggle slips over my lips. "Now you give me the words after you fill me up to the brim."

He chuckles right along with me and we both relish in the moment. The love, the devotion, the way our paths crossed and made everything line up to the point where we are right now; in love with our future wide open.

The years we have in our past are a promise for what's still to come. And I can't wait to explore every minute of it if it means I get to share it with Conroy and Baxter. Family. A brotherhood. Elements that link our lives and allow us the foundation to reach beyond our limits, knowing we will always have the support from one another.

It's just like Conroy said; loving is as easy as taking one breath after another. It doesn't require thinking, it's as natural as the sun rising and falling one day to the next. And my life might not be as perfect as those lines sound, but it's pretty damn close.

THANK YOU!

*Thank you for reading **"Two Silent Nights Times Two."** Kayler and Olcay's story **"Two Silent Nights"** is also available if you haven't read it yet!*

For more information on Addy's books, go to:
https://books2read.com/rl/AddyArcher

*For more information on
Esther E. Schmidt's books, go to:*
https://books2read.com/rl/esthereschmidt

SPECIAL THANKS

My beta team;
Neringa, Lynne, Wendy,

my pimp team, and to you, as my reader…
Thanks so much! You guys rock!

Contact:

We love hearing from my readers.

Email:

authoresthereschmidt@gmail.com

authoraddyarcher@gmail.com

Or contact Esther's PA **Christi Durbin** for any questions you might have.

facebook.com/CMDurbin

ESTHER E. SCHMIDT

Visit Esther E. Schmidt online:

Website:
www.esthereschmidt.nl

Facebook - AuthorEstherESchmidt
Twitter - @esthereschmidt
Instagram - @esthereschmidt
Pinterest - @esthereschmidt

Signup for Esther's newsletter:
esthereschmidt.nl/newsletter

Join Esther's fan group on Facebook:
www.facebook.com/groups/estherselite

ADDY ARCHER
WHERE SUSPENSE BLEEDS TO ROMANCE

Visit Addy Archer online:

Website:
www.addyarcher.com

Facebook - AuthorAddyArcher
Twitter - @AddyArcher
Instagram - @MCauthoraddy
TikTok - @AddyArcher

Signup for Addy's newsletter:
http://addyarcher.com/Newsletter.html

Join Addy's fan group on Facebook:
https://facebook.com/groups/AddyArchersRebels

MORE BOOKS

Esther E. Schmidt & Addy Archer

THE DUDNIK CIRCLE

PEACOCK
THE FAULTS OF OUR SINS

MARLON
NEON MARKSMAN MC

THE FALLON BROTHERS

UNRULY DEFENDERS MC

FREDERICK

UNRULY PROTECTOR

Swamp heads
SERIES

Printed in Great Britain
by Amazon